GOING WEST

Going West

Selected Stories

Normandi Ellis

*For Aneta
w/ Love & Friendship,*

WIND PUBLICATIONS

Normandi Ellis

Going West. Copyright © 2011 by Normandi Ellis. Printed in the United States of America. No part of this book may be reproduced in any manner without permission, except for brief quotations embodied in critical articles or reviews. For information, address Wind Publications, 600 Overbrook Drive, Nicholasville, KY 40356.

International Standard Book Number 978-1-936138-35-7
Library of Congress Control Number 2011925534

First edition

For my brothers,

Edward and Byron

ACKNOWLEDGEMENTS

Thanks to everybody who ever had to put up with me while I was writing these stories. They span such a long period of time now — and as one ages, things begin to take on that atmospheric blue seen in Renaissance paintings. I just want to say that if your life and mine intersected, I was blessed by it.

Thanks to the editors of the following journals where these stories first appeared:

"Dr. Livingston's Grotto," *Southern Humanities Review xxiii:3,* 1989.
"The Weight of the World," *Mediphors Journal* no. 10, 1997.
"Acting Lessons," *Southern Humanities Review* 34:1, 2000.
"Going West," *The Chaffin Journal,* 1998.
"Two More of the Same," *Westword,* 1989.
"Spiritualism," *Agni Review:* 27, 1988.
"Maytag," and "How Things Work" first appeared in *Sorrowful Mysteries and Other Stories* (Corvallis OR: Arrowood Books, 1991).

The author is grateful to the Kentucky Arts Council Al Smith Fellowship and the Kentucky Foundation for Women. Their generous financial support allowed time and opportunity for these stories to appear.

Cover photograph —
"Arches National Park" by Celeste Francis Pressley
<http://thecalicofox.com/landscapes.html>

TABLE OF CONTENTS

Dr. Livingston's Grotto	1
The Weight of the World	16
Temporarily Away	22
Maytag	32
Acting Lessons	52
Going West	67
The Gold in His Mouth	77
Papa in Pentimento	92
Fighting Poverty	121
Two More of the Same	127
Spiritualism	136
Real Estate	146

DR. LIVINGSTON'S GROTTO

One day while Dr. Livingston's wife sat inside their air-conditioned, ranch style house and while Dr. Livingston clomped in muddied boots about the garden, staking his tomato plants with Mrs. Livingston's worn out panty hose, the ground in their back yard opened up. It trembled a little, then yawned like a mouth, so that when Dr. Livingston turned toward the house, carrying his aluminum pie tin of ripe Better Boy tomatoes, he stepped unknowingly into the hole, and the earth surrounding it crumbled. He fell, slipping into the small fresh cave, and disappeared without a sound.

It was a gentle fall, which surprised him. He landed on his rump, knees bent. The cave's entrance had been no larger than the average manhole cover; and once past the slippery, narrow shaft, the whole thing opened up into a large, limestone room lit only by the slanted sunlight streaming in from the hole above. All else in the cave was black.

Dr. Livingston stood, brushed himself off, determined nothing was broken, and tried to figure out how to raise himself back to the surface. After the harsh sunlight of the upper world, his eyes were not yet accustomed to the dark. Not knowing whether he stood near the edge of a precipice, he was afraid to move very far one way or the other. When he stretched out his arms on either side, he could barely see his hands. He stooped down and felt the ground where he stood. There was no ledge behind him that he could find, and so he sat down again to think.

He reached to the right and discovered one of his tomatoes; at least he thought it was a tomato by its weight and the roundness of it. It seemed still to hold the warmth of the sun. He put it to his mouth and bit. Juice and seed dribbled down his chin. He wiped the mess off himself with his shirt tail. Then he took out his penknife and cut the tender meat into wedges. He glanced longingly toward the cave entrance where the sunlight trickled in. Oh, he thought, if I only had some salt.

"Help!" he shouted. "This is Dr. Livingston. Help me!"

The words echoed, tumbled, and roared. Long after he stopped shouting he thought he could still hear himself in some distant reaches of the cave. It must be an enormous place, he thought. If only I could see it. He reached into his pocket and withdrew a book of matches, striking one after the other, but the matches fizzled because of the dampness. At last one took hold and gave off a feeble glow, just enough for him to see, before the match burnt out, a large stalagmite to his left, jutting up like an ancient tooth.

"Incredible," he whispered.

"Credible," the cave whispered back.

He tilted his chin up, trying to direct his voice toward the hole above him because he imagined the sound on the surface would be pitifully weak, drowned out by bird song, lawn mowers, sprinklers.

"Help! Help! Down here."

He had orchestra practice this evening and he had promised to mow the lawn. There were the loose bathroom tiles he'd promised Flora he would caulk. He thought of a thousand things as if thinking them could draw him back to the surface. Surely it wouldn't be long before someone heard him, or Flora called him to supper, or Ted Waterfield missed him at this evening's practice, or, barring any of the above, a neighbor heard his cry.

"Help. This is Dr. Livingston," he called again.

"Stun. Stun," the cave answered.

Inside Dr. Livingston's tightly sealed, air-conditioned house, Mrs. Livingston sat with three friends, equally as large as she, playing bridge and munching Lorna Doones held delicately between their thumbs and forefingers. Before each bid, she smoothed the skirt of her peach dress, fingered the pearls lying on her ample chest, and patted the bobby pins back into her bun.

"Three hearts," she said.

Her partner, Mrs. Waterfield, raised her right eyebrow and cleared her throat. They were cheating, of course, passing signals back and forth like baseball players, but if the other two women knew it, they said nothing.

"Pass," said Mrs. King, biting her cookie.

Between bids all that could be heard was the low hum of the air conditioner. Usually, whenever Mrs. Livingston held a bridge party, her husband came in under the auspices of looking for something — a pan, a screwdriver, or some other excuse — just so he could stand over her shoulder and peek at her cards. She thought it was nice that George had found something else to occupy himself this afternoon.

Dr. Livingston sat cross-legged amid the rubble that had fallen down with him. It was a wonder he hadn't been killed. He had heard of cows falling into such sinkholes. Of course, Bowling Green was riddled with caves, but he hadn't counted on having one open in his back yard. He wondered if his homeowner's insurance considered such things as acts of God.

His glow-in-the-dark watch read 2:47, the same time it read when last he checked it. He held it to his ear, shook it, and at last, pulled it from his wrist and flung it. The odd thing was that he did not hear it land, and he could hear everything in the cave, even his breath. It must have fallen into a hole and dropped a long way down. He wondered whether he was sitting on the edge of a huge precipice.

At first the cave had seemed thick with darkness, but as his eyes adjusted, he could see on the ceiling, just beneath where the sunlight angled in, a cluster of calcium carbonate deposits hanging like beads of pearls. It was beautiful, really; and it seemed odd to think that such a geologic wonder had been forming for centuries beneath his feet, that for all the gardens he had planted and lawns he had mowed, for all the farms tilled and bulldozers turning forest to subdivisions, for all the highways and office buildings laid through the city that the earth had maintained its secret life, a life that went on deep within despite everything.

"Help! Flora!" he called. "Get me out!"

"Me out. Me out. Me out."

Finally he gave up calling and stretched out on the limestone floor. He would have to wait until someone came looking for him.

The afternoon drew itself out like a long sigh. The sun moved west, growing heavier, falling in a slow arc from its zenith. The light in the cave grew dimmer. Dr. Livingston got up on his hands and knees, crawling slowly across the slick limestone floor and, groping in the dark, managed to gather the rest of his tomatoes. He was eating them one by one, calling for help in different voices between each bite.

"Help," he whispered, then "He-elp," he said in a low, rumbling voice. "Halp!" he squeaked.

He listened to the voices echoing back to him. It was only a game now, something to help pass the time. He wondered how long it would take Flora to miss him. Then he lay back silent, cradling his head in his hands, and stared up at the hole again. The blue in the sky deepened; the light began to fade. To his amazement he saw eight pale stars embedded in the afternoon sky, and it occurred to him that they had been at his back all the while he had been staking tomatoes in his garden.

"How clever is the world," he said, "to conceal its wonder."

"Wonder," the cave agreed.

Inside the cave it was quiet, really quiet, like a cathedral (or a crypt, he thought). He listened to his breath, his heart beat, the tomatoes churning in his stomach. He could hear the monotonous drip, drip, drip of water somewhere that sounded like a metronome. Dr. Livingston began to sing.

In the mines, in the mines, in the Blue Diamond mines,
I have worked my life away.
In the mines, in the mines, in the Blue Diamond mines,
Oh, fall on your knees and pray ...

His baritone reverberated through the cave. It sounded quite good. He wished he had the whole orchestra down there. If he ever got to the surface again, he decided, he might invite Waterfield and a few of the others in. What a chorus that would make.

He began to wish he had some Rossini down there in the hole with him. He slapped his thighs beating out the time to The Thieving Magpie. "Ba-ba-ba bah ba bum!" It appeared he would miss orchestra practice this evening. He looked up toward the hole again. Yes, it was definitely getting darker.

"Help!" he called, but his heart wasn't quite in it. He was thinking about Rossini. "Ta-ta-ta-ta-ta-ta-ta-ta-ta teedle-de-de," he sang.

The time passed. The sun set. It was black as coal inside the cave. In the seven hours since his fall, Dr. Livingston had played upon his now sore and burning thighs the music of Rossini, Vivaldi, and Beethoven, with a little John Philip Sousa thrown in for good measure.

"George? George?"

He paused in the midst of song. He thought he heard a voice somewhere. It seemed to come from miles away.

"George, where are you?"

He cupped his hands around his mouth, directing his voice upward. "Down here!" he shouted. "Flora, help me!"

"Where?"

"Here, this hole. Watch out."

But of course, she wouldn't fall in — Mrs. Livingston was too wide. He saw several flashes of light, then the beam appeared directly above him with Mrs. Livingston's face beside it.

"What are you doing down there?"

"Singing."

"Well, come on now. Your chicken's getting cold."

"I can't," he said. "I can't get back up. I fell into this hole. It's some sort of cave, part of the Mammoth Cave system, I'd venture to guess. Throw me down the flashlight and call someone for help."

She threw it down — it hit the stone floor with a clatter — and ran back toward the house. Dr. Livingston picked up the flashlight and bounced its beams on the walls around him. To his left, row upon row of stalagmites spiraled into the air, some of them reaching up and melding with the stalactites that dripped from above. He put out his hand and touched one. It was cool and slick and wet. There must have been iron deposits in the water, as the stone spires appeared rather orange and yellow in color.

He shined the light to his right where a narrow passageway snaked off into the darkness. He followed, crawling on his belly until it began to twist downward. He stopped where the tunnel dipped sharply and turned right over a mound of flowstone. Not wanting to lose himself in the dark, he inched himself backward. Without the sun, he would be hard-pressed to find the cave entrance again. He sat again in the cavernous room and waited for Flora.

"George! George!"

"Flora! Here!"

It took a while for them to locate each other in the dark. At last she appeared with a second flashlight.

"They say they can't come until morning."

"You mean I have to spend the night down here? Good God!"

Mrs. Livingston began to wail. He hated it when she cried. It was bad enough to have to listen to it; he was glad he couldn't see her eyes welling up with tears and her wet lower lip jutting out, trembling like a fat child's.

"Listen to me. Stop crying, for Pete's sake. It won't do any good. If I have to spend the night down here, could you at least bring me some dinner, a pillow, and a blanket?"

"And how am I supposed to get all that down?"

"Think Flora. There's a rope in the shed. Tie the stuff to the rope and lower it down."

She disappeared from the hole. He thought for a moment, then shouted. "Flora! Flora, wait!"

She came back.

"What?"

A smile crept over his lips. "Could you bring me my saxophone?"

The things he needed appeared one by one. First, Mrs. Livingston dropped down one of Dr. Livingston's old army blankets. It hit him on the head. Then the pillow appeared, followed by the rope which, inch by inch, lowered a bucket of Colonel Sanders' Kentucky Fried Chicken, complete with greasy biscuit and a little Styrofoam cup of cold mashed potatoes and gravy.

"Sakes, Flora! I thought you made chicken," he said.

"I didn't have time. You know when you didn't come in after so long, we played another hand and then another."

"Well, who won?"

"I did," she said. "Just like always."

"You cheat."

There was a pause. "Yes," she said. "I have to defend my position."

She would never have admitted to such a thing if he hadn't been trapped in a cave. His situation must have seemed to her a matter of grave importance.

"You shouldn't cheat, Flora. It isn't nice," he said.

There came another silence. He could feel the bulk of her above his head, thinking. The tiny thoughts struggled up through the layers of Lorna Doones. He shivered. It frightened him to think of such a thing.

"Now, careful with my saxophone."

She tied the rope to the case handle and slowly, slowly it came down toward his outstretched hand, spinning a little on its length of rope. He untied it and gave a tug which signaled Mrs. Livingston to haul the rope back up.

He flung open the case, threw the strap around his neck, and clipped his instrument onto it, then he wet his lips, sucked the reed, and gently began to blow. Closing his eyes he breathed out a long hollow note that sighed and hung in the air all around him, echoing clear to infinity. By God, he thought, in the bowels of the earth a man could really play the blues. He began again faster this time, higher; the sounds rolled one over the other. He played what was in his head — all those years the melodies he had strained to remember when he woke from a dream, the sounds he could never quite catch before through the din of afternoon traffic. He heard them now and played. It felt wonderful, as if he were flying in the dark.

He stopped to listen to the last note reverberating off the walls.

"You haven't heard a word I've said," his wife complained. "You've been tooting that old thing the whole time. What I said was … I said to him, 'But you've got come now and get him out. He can't stay in there all night.' Then he said, 'Lady, I work from nine to five. If you want him out, drive your car into the back yard, tie a rope to it, and haul him out …'"

"Flora," he cried. "Listen very carefully. I need your help. Go into the house and get my notebook and paper."

"What?"

"I said …"

"I know what you said. What on earth for?"

"Flora, please!"

Oh, why did she make him beg? She was like an irritable, petulant mother, whining after him all the time, making him repeat everything he said.

"And bring me a beer or two, will you? There's nothing down here to drink. Just bring the whole six-pack. I'll be sleeping down here by myself on these rocks all night…. It's the least you could do."

"Oh, all right."

The flashlight went away and she with it. Dr. Livingston sat beneath the cave entrance looking up through the hole. It must have been a beautiful night above him. He saw his stars twinkling in the small patch of sky above. It was as if all the rest of the universe had gone away but for the stars that he could see. It reminded him of when he was a little boy and used to camp out in his back yard at night. He put the saxophone to his lips and blew again.

In a moment his wife returned and lowered the beer, pencil, and paper, which she'd tied in a plastic grocery bag to the end of the rope.

"Now the rope," he said.

"What!"

"I said the rope."

"I know what you said. But that man said we could tie it to the car and pull you up. I mean we could try it…."

"It won't work," he said, thinking fast. "Use your head, woman. If I just stepped into this whole, then the top must be very thin. Why, the weight of the car could cave the whole thing in on me. The whole house might fall in tomorrow! You could fall in yourself any minute." There was silence above him. He could tell she was thinking very hard about something, probably all the Lorna Doones she had eaten. She was trying to wish herself small.

"Now, throw me the rope."

She was reluctant to give it to him. It was the umbilicus that brought him food and drink; it was their only connection.

"There's a huge crevice here," he lied. "I'll have to tie myself to this ledge to sleep."

She dropped the rope to him.

"But, I'm not leaving you, George. If I have to sleep out in the grass with the crickets. I'm not…"

"Fine," he muttered.

He threw the light onto the cave walls, found the tunnel, then crawled through, pushing the saxophone and plastic bag ahead of him. When he reached the tunnel's end, he saw a huge yellow stalagmite beside the mound of flowstone. He tied one end of the rope to it and the other end to his waist. With the saxophone and plastic bag in one hand and the flashlight in the other, he lowered himself over the flowstone and slid a long way on his rump until his feet touched solid stone beneath him. He walked a few feet and came, as they say, to the end of his rope where he saw that he was, in fact, on a rather small ledge no more than three feet wide. Within reach he saw a green florescent glow and thinking it a rock, he picked it up. It was his watch, and it still read 2:47. He flung it even farther.

Below him he heard a lyrical, hollow, gurgling sound, and flashing his electric beam, located a stream. He glanced about, realizing this second cavern was more enormous than the first. It was, he thought, like a mammoth concert hall with vaulted ceilings and numerous entrances and exits. He tossed the light about him and discovered that if he walked carefully along the edge to his left, there was a passage down to the bank beside the stream.

For a moment he stood hesitating, glancing at the tether that led back up, then he untied himself, letting the rope dangle. He walked sideways with his chest against the wall until he arrived at the edge of the stream.

Out of the corner of his eye, he caught several silver flashes and turned his light full upon them in the water. A school of small, thin fish, no bigger than his finger, darted about the stream. The light did not seem to bother them and upon closer inspection, when he hovered over the clear water for a better look, he saw that they were both albino and blind — not just blind, but eyeless. Where the flat discs of their eyes should have been was a slight indentation, nothing more, and through their pale, delicate skin he perceived the fine, curved outline of their bones. He put his hand in the cold water and the fish darted away, as if somehow they felt his presence.

"Incredible," he whispered.

"Credible," the cave whispered back.

He opened the case, strapped the saxophone about his neck, and turned off the flashlight. He wore the damp, cool darkness like a second skin. He felt not himself, rather he felt ultimate, as if the infinite melodies that might arise from his fingers and breath burned and twisted through him like dark fire. He closed his eyes and blew. In the darkness it seemed that he was creating worlds.

Time passed, but it was geologic time; he did not bother to measure it. At first, he had tried stopping after each song to catch the flow with pen and paper; eventually he gave that up. Invariably a new note rushed in to fill the empty space of the last. It was one song and he played it for all he was worth. After a while, he stopped playing altogether until at last, he emptied himself out and all he could hear was the hollow gurgling of the stream and the metronome of the cave dripping.

He must have fallen asleep. Dr. Livingston stood and stretched himself. He wondered what time it was. Inside him there were more songs, but they were smothered by the rumbling in his stomach which meant that he was hungry. Flora's chicken dinner lay on the other side of the flowstone wall in the room upstairs. Mortal after all, he found his way back up the ledge to the rope hanging over the flowstone. It was more difficult this time — he was climbing uphill and had to keep both hands on the rope. He left the saxophone on the ledge and held the flashlight in his teeth.

Slowly, he inched his way up past the slick wall of mineral deposits and through the narrow tunnel until he came to the last turn. There, he noticed coming toward him a faint light, which surprised him. He switched off the flashlight and crawled toward it. When he entered the room, he saw with near-blinding clarity that it was day again and sunlight poured through the open pit, shining on the opposite wall.

Strangest of all, he spied upon his army blanket, a pinkish white, eyeless newt that lay basking in what must have seemed to it the sudden in-flowing warmth. its feathery red gills pumped fresh oxygen into its system as it held its skinny self up on spindly legs. It looked no more than a white pencil with appendages. Dr. Livingston watched its red gills flutter in the sunlight it could not see, and it seemed a sad sight to him, this abrupt change in the cave's environment. Perhaps in several hundred years the newt and fish would grow eyes again. Perhaps they would come, as their ancestors must have done, to rely on sight, forgetting the world of vibration and sound. He wanted to shield it — it seemed so naïve, so embryonic — to protect it from the ever encroaching outer world.

Dr. Livingston sat quietly in the far corner, watching the newt and eating his cold fried chicken. As soon as he was through, he would go back to his music and the stream. There seemed important work to do now. Very important. He might one day emerge himself, white-headed and blind, with a sheaf of music the likes of which no one else had ever heard. He would write what he could remember, and what he could not remember ... well, he would have played it and that would have to be enough for any reasonable man.

He paused in mid-bite of his chicken thigh and stared again at the pale, slick creature on the blanket. It seemed to tremble visibly, then in a moment, it darted away into the dark recesses of the cave. He wondered what could have frightened it. In the next moment he felt it, too — a low rumbling that shook the ground, growing louder and louder, shaking him. The chicken thigh slipped from his hand. Somewhere he heard rocks falling and thought of his beautiful orange stone icicles shattering on the cavern floor.

"No!" he shouted. "Go back!"

The truck roared through Dr. Livingston's back yard, across his tomato plants and stopped near the edge of the sinkhole. Mrs. Livingston spluttered and cried, waving her handkerchief. Four men leaped from the truck — a doctor with his black medical bag; two technicians in tan jumpsuits, who began removing ropes and lanterns and oxygen tanks from the truck; and an official-looking young man in a brown suit and tie. The green bullhorn tired to his belt loop swung like a pendulum as he flung his hand, snapping his fingers at the technicians, and pointing down the hole.

"All night I called to him," Mrs. Livingston wailed. "Talked to him, but he didn't answer. Oh God, do something! He's dead down there, suffocated or fallen or broken a leg or something."

The official young man spread his handkerchief over the grass to prevent a stain on his pants and, leaning over the edge of the precipice, shouted, "Dr. Livingston. This is Robert C. Cunningham, Jr. of the Commonwealth of Kentucky, Department of Parks and Recreation, Geological Investigation Division. Can you hear me, sir!"

"Yeah, I hear you," Dr. Livingston grumbled. "Your damn truck scared my newt."

He bit into his chicken thigh again, thinking hard. The bullhorn started in once more.

"Dr. Livingston. This is Robert C. Cunningham, Jr. of the Commonwealth's Department of Parks and Recreation. We're coming in for a rescue, sir. Don't panic. I repeat, do not ..."

"Hold it! Hold it!" Dr. Livingston shouted. "I'm right here and I can hear you fine. You don't need to blast my ears off with that thing. It echoes like crazy in here. What's the matter with you? Haven't you ever been in a cave before?"

There was a short pause and then it seemed as if the sun's light were cut away from him. He thought for a moment that they had sealed him in, then he realized it was only Mrs. Livingston leaning over the hole.

"Tarnation, George! Why didn't you answer me last night? You scared the pee out of me!"

"Dr. Livingston. This cave is the property of the Commonwealth of Kentucky and off limits to the general populace …"

"What do you mean Commonwealth? This is my back yard. As far as you know this cave wasn't even here twenty-four hours ago. Who the devil do you think you are?"

"This is Robert C. Cunningham, Jr. I'm a speleologist with the Commonwealth of Kentucky, Department of …"

"All right. All right," he shouted back.

"We've come to extricate you from the cave. Sir."

"Who needs it? Just throw me a couple of ropes over the edge…."

"You don't know what you are doing. You can fall, Dr. Livingston. Fall and die."

"So?"

"George, please. They're here to save you. Oh, what's the matter with him? Don't be stupid, George."

He muttered, gathering up his fried chicken box, his blanket, and pillow, tidying the cave.

"We'll throw you a rope. Tie it around your waist. I repeat … Tie it around your waist. And we will haul you up."

"Well, wait just a minute," Dr. Livingston said. "I have to go back for my saxophone."

"His what?" the speleologist muttered to Mrs. Livingston.

"Saxophone. I don't know. He made me bring it to him."

Dr. Livingston tied his rope around his waist again and bellycrawled back through the tunnel toward the larger chamber below. This time he didn't need the flashlight. It was as if, twisting and turning, he could maneuver the narrow tunnel blind. Good as the damn newt, he told himself. He reached the flowstone and tied the rope to the stalagmite, then lowered himself down.

He reached out his hand slowly, feeling in the dark. A few feet away from him on the ledge, he located his saxophone. The case felt cool and eager for his touch. For a long time, Dr. Livingston stood in the dark, listening to the stream, smelling the damp, earthy cave smell, and tapping his foot tentatively to the monotonous drip, drip, drip of the cave.

"Bah-bum-pum-pum-pum," he sang softly.

"Bah-bum," the cave answered.

Dr. Livingston reached into his pocket, pulled out his penknife, and cut the rope, then lowered himself into the main cavity. He clapped his hands in the darkness.

"Go now!" he urged the fish and his newt.

"Go now," the cave said.

He wished that he could crawl off with them down one of the unexplored tunnels. He thought of the wonders he would know, the music he could play; but he knew that sooner or later they would find him, and his heart cleaved like an ancient stone.

He sat by the stream, found a half-full beer, and finished it off; then he opened his case, slung the saxophone around his neck, and wet his lips. He blew into it slowly. It was a sweet cry — a baleful, beautiful, resonant sound. He sat quietly a moment, listening to its echo. Music flowed through his veins like dark water, etching out secret caverns, filling him with wonder.

In this world, thought Dr. Livingston, there were just some things a man had to do. Then he licked his lips and breathed the song again.

THE WEIGHT OF THE WORLD

I wasn't sure what I saw. Something high-flown and falling through the air. A flimsy bit of plastic, a gray sheet escaped from the laundry, a falling cloud. The woman rolled over the hood of the car ahead of me, then off its back. She landed in the street. It took a while for the image to register. I was daydreaming, queued up at the stop light fifteen feet away from the accident, perhaps closer or farther; I can't remember. Everything appeared startlingly near yet far away. I think the car had emerged from the cross-traffic and was turning left. But I didn't see it coming. Perhaps my imagination had to invent that left-hand turn to crystallize the fact of the accident. After the impact, came a moment of hesitation, a period of slow dawning disbelief, and then the gray sedan stopped.

The pedestrian lay on the ground, the last fluttering folds of cloth draping themselves over her stockinged legs before I recognized the gathering shape was a woman. Slowly I made out the details. Gray calf-length raincoat, long dish-water blond hair. The light, my light, was red. She lay in the street in front of me, or perhaps in the bus lane. Not quite off the curb, but not quite on. She had hit her head on something — I wasn't sure what I saw — the curb perhaps. She was not moving. Definitely not moving.

Now that I think about it, there were no sounds. No cry. No screech of tires. No violent thuds. Nothing. Everything hung suspended from the sky by invisible threads. Another woman stood very still, absolutely still, in the middle of the crosswalk, holding her purse, clutching her umbrella. It had been raining off and on all day, a misty kind of rain that drivers want to hurry through in order to get home to hot tea or a fire. The on-looker kept looking, frozen red lips, black eyes, trapped in a moment in time. She was dark-haired, with bangs, wore a tan raincoat. She may have been walking with the victim, perhaps they'd been telling those distracted after-work-day stories of cloaked desperation, and then when she'd turned for affirmation, her friend was gone. I don't know this, of course. I have to invent it. But I am absolutely sure of the expression on that woman's face as she turned to look into the emptiness, clutching her umbrella. It was a look of abandonment, of surprise.

The woman lay in the street. The light was still red and I sat in my car. A cream-colored over-the-shoulder purse lay on the ground, its broken strap a snake slithering along the slick pavement. Perhaps eight feet away lay a brightly colored green umbrella, closed and folded on itself. Emerald green, the color of jungle leaves. I believe it belonged to the victim and had been wrenched from her hand by the blow. The purse lay so near, the umbrella so far, the woman immobile as I contemplated these things.

My fingers clenched the steering wheel. I wondered what I should do. None of my instincts seemed right. I wondered idly if I could still make a right hand turn on the red light since no other cars were coming. I wondered if I should flick on the hazard lights and dash across the street. Perhaps other cars were coming after all. Any moment the red light would change. I sat in my car and wondered if the woman were dead, if this was the day that I would see someone die like an animal while I watched, if I would be able to live with myself afterward, knowing I'd done nothing. I did not look away. I did not move. The light was still red. Perhaps an hour had passed, perhaps only a few seconds.

I became angry. I was angry with whoever it was who could run over a pedestrian, then sit and do nothing. The world is a fragile thing. It holds together only by our concentration on it. A moment of inattention, and a whole life could disappear. Why did the driver continue to sit? Why was the car still running, poised in the middle of the street, puffing soft white wisps of exhaust, while the poor woman lay sprawled on the asphalt behind the rear wheels where the frozen terrified eyes staring into the rear view mirror could not see what damage had been done? I remember those eyes — dark, dazed, and animal. I do not know if they were male or female. Why did the driver not fling open the car door? Why didn't I? And still the light was red.

A chill seized me when I realized that until that fateful fluttering and falling, neither had I seen the pedestrian and her companion enter the crosswalk. In that moment panic set in, and I became terrified that it was not the other driver, but I who had done it. I had hit her and broken her and caused this woman to lie immobile on the ground. The day was utterly gray. All of us should have turned on our headlights, even though dark was still an hour away. All of us should have checked our brakes. All of us out walking should have worn reflective tape and carried bright umbrellas. Perhaps it was the woman who had not seen the car and stepped in front of it. I hadn't seen it. Was its color gray? I remember only the eyes in the mirror, the rolled up windows, closed doors, the engine idling. I could not say truly what color it was, what model or make, what license plate. I could not see the driver who did not move, did not blink, but who nevertheless at that moment was as much a victim of the accident as the fallen pedestrian.

And still the light hung red upon a black wire. And the woman lay on the street. Where were the policemen? And why didn't somebody do something?

I had just come from my friend Veronica's house where we'd been talking over tea in shuttered rooms perfumed with rose petals, dried orange peel and clove. I often visit Veronica — she's bright and witty, beautiful and sensitive, and she tells me stories. I've been dropping by more often ever since last month when she told me she was going to kill herself. We were in her garden, dead-heading the flowers; I was pinching & collecting seeds to plant this spring.

"Oh, you don't mean that," I said lightly. The sky was the blue of a robin's egg and the clouds were high and wispy.

"Actually," she said. "I've been planning it for many years." She pulled the garden shears from her pocket and began snipping at roses. The few remaining blossoms that fell to the ground Veronica didn't bother to gather. She executed the living and the dead without regard, saying she'd made a list of everything she needed to do first: make a will, buy a cemetery plot, buy a gun, ask her roommate to move, pay her bills, disconnect the phone ...

Of course, I did not think she would do it. Veronica and I often have speculative kinds of discussions. "It's just winter coming on," I said. "You're feeling fragile."

"Quite the opposite," she said. "I feel stronger than I have in some time. I'm quite sure about this. There is no reason to live." She took one of my cigarettes and lit it, even though three months before she'd given up smoking. She squinted at me in the haze that drifted between us. "We are trapped inside our bodies. And the burden of it is unbearable." Her face was placid while she spoke, but when she said goodbye, the single unstifled tear seeping from her eye frightened me.

Now a month had passed, Veronica tucked her list in the drawer of her roll top desk. She says she is feeling better. "But still," she said today, "I believe that this physical form is a trap for the spiritual. And I'm not relinquishing my option to let go of this existence, if I so choose." She contemplated the long ash on the end of her cigarette before flicking it toward the ashtray. The ashes flew into a confetti of gray dust on the mirrored table.

"Veronica," I said. "There is really nowhere to go. This body. This rocking chair. The cars we drive. The food we eat. The plastic ashtrays in front of us, for Chris'sake ... they're all made of ensnared forms of energy, random particles of light held together, by what? Perhaps mutual consent. Even the thoughts we think, the sparks between synapses, all fizzles of light. There's no place to go but back to it. Energy can never be destroyed. It merely disperses and transforms. Don't you see? You can't really leave, no matter how hard you try."

She stubbed the cigarette out in the ashtray and leaned back in her rocker. A single ray of light crept between the clouds and the shuttered window landing inside the filthy amber ashtray in Veronica's otherwise perfectly ordered house. "It's not that I don't believe in God," she said, "or some ultimate truth, but it all falls apart faster than we can sweep up the pieces. It's such a cruel trick," she said. "Sometimes I can't bear it."

I left reluctantly, which is how I always leave Veronica. It's not a shameful thing to say that I love her. I wish I'd taken her list and thrown it away. I wanted to stay her destroying hand and tell Veronica that energy is divine, that she is light itself, a spark, a current dancing between two poles.

My mind felt so crowded with these almost tangible thoughts that as I drove away through the rain-slicked streets, I was sure Veronica could feel me thinking them. I cruised down Main Street, talking to myself, distractedly, imagining talking to Veronica, probably even wildly gesturing as I do when thoughts get too big to contain simply in a mind. I was thinking how much I wanted to turn around right then, drive back to her house and tell her that we are the forms of god, the only way god has of experiencing itself. What if I was right, what if that meant that nothing was any more tangible than air, what if none of us were real ... then none of it mattered, nothing mattered, not the pain, not even the joy.

I stopped at the red light, looking left quickly before making a right hand turn. In truth, I did not see the accident. I saw nothing but Veronica's sad and golden face burning its way through my mind. Out of the corner of my eye I saw the woman fall. At first I thought it was a sack of garbage floating oddly on the wind in imitation of an angel. I realize now it was a mortal woman. She lay unmoving, and around her everything stopped. The cars. The pedestrians, the lights, the clouds. Perhaps she lay unconscious on the asphalt and we, like inert bits of ash, waited for her to awaken, to concentrate her energies and bring us back to focus, or to blow the bits of scattered dust so that, at last, unleashed from the heavy curse of the unknowable truth, we could move along our way. And I sat in the car — spinning, waiting, a moment of absolute emptiness. And the light was red.

Then the woman's arm crept out from under the tangle of hair. A man standing on the sidewalk across the street — had he been there all this time? — a man in khaki pants, dark-haired, with brown tasseled shoes ran into the intersection past the frozen woman who stood still clutching her purse.

At last the woman pushed one arm beneath herself and tried to rise. The man lifted her slowly. The friend frozen in the intersection began to move. The fallen woman got up, stumbled and shook her head. "Still alive!" I whispered. The light turned green. I felt a solitary dampness on my cheek like a single raindrop. The cars began to move, angling themselves carefully and slowly around the stray green umbrella, which still lay in the middle of the intersection, advertising the weight of the world.

TEMPORARILY AWAY

Standing outside the closet door I hold my father's tweed hat, the one with the leather sweat band that smells like Old Spice, the one with the small red feather tucked into the outer band. There's a two-finger crease in the crown, although over the last few years of sitting on the shelf, the brim has curled slightly. Papa wore this hat when he went to the racetrack, sporting Mama in gold earrings on his arm.

During Keeneland's spring meet, rows of redbuds blossomed along the outer loops of the track. The tiny pink flowers outlined each tree branch — sometimes bursting out along the tree spine as if the flowers were joyfully escaping. My father always bet the fifth horse in the fifth race. He almost never won. Between races, my parents leaned against the rail outside the paddock while hot-walkers made the rounds parading their sleek thoroughbreds. Encouraging Papa to bet a different horse, I suggested that statistically the sixth horse wins more often because it is less likely to be trapped against the rail. I showed Papa a column of figures I'd averaged in red ink on the back of the racing form. He said my analysis only proved that it was I who did not like the feeling of being trapped.

For my parents, it wasn't about the Keeneland carousel; it was about sunshine, redbuds, and the flutter of tickets at day's end. Life's possibilities seemed limitless, like the gin and tonics that flowed from the clubhouse.

After Papa's strokes and heart attack, the dementia crept in. Mama's stress escalated until she was in the emergency room more often than Papa. Going from panic to hysteria, she found herself one day standing in Papa's closet with a pair of scissors, shredding the pants he could never hang up right. After her stamping and shrieking, it became obvious to us all that the safest place for Papa was away.

Mama invited me to witness Papa's in-home evaluation by a veterans' center nurse. When he dressed that day he'd managed to scoop most of his shirt tail inside his pants, although he kept on his bathrobe because the house was too cold. The nurse started with simple questions. She asked what day it was. Papa guessed Monday. "Every day feels like Monday," he said.

She asked him how long he'd been married. He halted.

Mama said, "Forty-eight years."

The nurse suggested that it might be best if Papa answered the questions. She asked him how many children he had.

"Four," he said.

Behind his back Mama held up three fingers.

"Three? Or four?" asked the nurse.

Papa said, "Four." Mama chimed in, "Three."

Papa said, "Well, yes... Bette and I have three children." He hesitated, thinking. "Then there's the little girl."

What girl? My daughter, or some other little girl I didn't know about?

"Who is the president?" the nurse asked.

"Things are such a mess," he answered, thinking hard. "It must be a Republican."

The nurse laughed. Papa was funny. Papa was charming, but it was Wednesday, Bill Clinton was in office, and Papa had three children. I realized he had been faking it for a long time. I knew Mama needed to be relieved of this responsibility, but I wished she hadn't sat on the sofa and smiled as if she'd just won a prize on Jeopardy.

A week later Mama called to say that Papa had moved into Wilmore.

"How did he seem when he left?" I asked.

"Like he was ready…. He packed his suitcases with a little help and carried them down the sidewalk to the car. He was just like a soldier going off to war. He never even looked back."

I imagined him wearing his tweed hat, his overcoat flapping open, his shoulders stooped a little from the weight of two suitcases. So many times I'd seen him traveling down the sidewalk that way. It might have seemed like another business trip, but this time he'd been called by the Veteran's Administration and he would go where they sent him.

When I stand in the closet holding Papa's hat, I close my eyes and breathe in the scent of my father. I can almost smell dust, the sunlight on the track, and the combined scents of gin and tonic and sweat. I can almost hear him whistling and jingling the car keys as he strolls down the sidewalk of my memory. "Temporarily away," I tell myself as I so often said in childhood. I return the hat to its shelf and close the closet door.

At the nursing home Papa sat at the table with a tray pressed close to his chest. Squeezed into this tight spot at the table, Papa could barely raise his hands as he tried to eat gray scrambled eggs with a plastic spoon. When he finally saw me, he dropped the spoon and wiggled two fingers like an ant telegraphing a message with its antennae. I wiggled my fingers back.

"Finish those eggs and I'll buy you a milkshake," I said.

"Are we going somewhere?"

"We're just going for a drive," I said. "The redbuds are in bloom."

He stared at me open-mouthed. Sometimes it seemed he had forgotten how to breathe. I watched the thoughts bubble up as if struggling through the thick gray porridge that was his brain.

"Am I going home?" he asked and waited while the next thought surfaced. "They said I'm fine and I can go home now."

I got up, scooted my chair under the Formica table, and turned away. "I'll just check you out for the day, Papa, and get your medicine."

At the nurses' station I signed for the receipt of two huge plastic bags of medicine and received my instructions on how and when to give it. The nurses told me that he had packed all of his clothes and books into boxes. "He thinks he is going home." They wondered if I should be taking him out. I promised that I wouldn't let him out of the car.

I rolled Papa's wheelchair through the metal gate, took him down the elevator and we traveled the dark corridor toward the front door. My sandals clopped and the sound rang in my ears. I walked faster. Clop-clop, clop-clop. My heart pumped like a thoroughbred's heart headed into the home stretch. I couldn't wait to jump the gate, to get outside. My own voice screamed in my head, "Go, go, go!" I hurried toward the sunlight, across the shiny floors, across the waxed and dried bright yellow pee stains. The fluorescent lights flickered overhead. The hydraulic doors hissed and burst open like an exploding heart.

Suddenly standing on the sidewalk in front of the building where the nurses took their cigarette breaks, I stopped and breathed. Their fetid air smelled better than the hallways reeking of urine and forgetfulness.

I drove away quickly. We left behind pureed vegetables, milk cartons, and paper napkins tucked under sagging chins. I drove the back roads with their green hills full of thoroughbreds, along a creek where purple and white larkspur blanketed the limestone cliffs. "Look," I said, pointing to wildflowers and the redbuds springing up between the rows of green cedars. We used to travel the back roads like this when I was a kid. I didn't want my father to forget this beautiful world.

"Are we home yet?" Papa asked. "I want to see my mother."

In 1978 I stood on the sidewalk with a red stocking cap tugged down to my eyebrows while the weak November sun rose through bare tree branches. Yellow sweet gum leaves lay wet and sizzling in the front lawn, as if overnight the sky had fallen into the grass.

"You don't know what you're doing," Mama shouted. You're killing your father!"

I'd been leaving for months; I'd been leaving all year. I'd been leaving ever since I was born. Standing on the sidewalk in front of my childhood home, I felt pretty good. I'd finally quit waking up and wondering what I was supposed to do with my life. Inside the twelve cardboard boxes in my car, I also carried the certainty that my future existed out west somewhere.

"You'll be back," Mama shouted. "You won't last six weeks."

Sweating profusely and on his way to work, Papa nearly bulged out of his suit jacket. A small vial of nitroglycerin tablets formed a familiar lump in his shirt pocket. I hugged him. I waited for him to say something profound.

"Write when you find work," he said.

I threw myself into the car — a bright blue car the color of a robin's egg cracked open. I knew that if I didn't leave right then, I might fall down on the sidewalk and stay there forever. I'd been dreaming that a stranger had been living my life in Colorado. The time had come for me to drive west, wrest my life away from her, and reclaim it.

"You may never see us again," Mama warned. "We are old."

I got into my car, blew kisses and drove twenty-five hours straight into tomorrow. Outside Denver the sun came up blasting bright rays onto the Flatirons that jutted straight out of the earth into the western sky. I pulled off the roadway and turned to see the blazing sunrise behind me in the eastern sky. For fourteen years I watched the sunrise that way, but my bravado didn't last.

After the divorce my daughter and I came back home.

When I'd visited Papa in the middle of November, he seemed eager to recount his latest outing. I hadn't seen him this animated in a long time and hoped that this was an improvement. Papa said that recently the nurses and doctors had loaded the patients onto a tour bus bound for the race track. Doubt settled in me. Would the nursing staff really take a tour bus full of dementia patients someplace where they could walk off?

"It was just amazing," Papa said, telling me how he'd ridden on the bus with the film crew. They'd interviewed him the whole time.

"A film crew!" I said with surprise. "What did they interview you about?"

"This and that," he said.

I wheeled Papa's chair down the scuff-marked corridor toward the solitary patch of sunlight in the courtyard of the nursing home. Although the day was chilly, I wanted to sit in strong sunlight where I could lift my chin, close my eyes, and talk to my father without smelling feces or burned bean soup.

"So what did you say exactly?" I asked.

"Well, I told them all about my life in Louisville and about the plays I wrote during the war. They had seen my plays on Broadway, of course ..."

"I didn't know you had plays on Broadway."

"Everybody on the crew was so wonderful," Papa recalled. "They want me to star in a movie called *My Old Kentucky Life*." Papa's hands fluttered like birds into his lap as he nodded to himself, remembering it. "Of course, I told them my mother has to play the violin." His eyes grew misty at the thought of seeing his life made into a movie and his mother playing the film score. "And everybody was so wonderful. We were all so happy to know that you will be writing the script." His mouth drooped into an "O." "It was just wonderful," he repeated, choking up. "And I'm so happy, so very happy."

Snot dripped from the tip of his nose, or perhaps tears. I dug in my purse for tissues. The tissues were easy to find; Papa's mind not so much.

I had thought my father's absence would lighten Mama's load. Instead, she began to isolate herself inside her brick house with the drapes closed, hiding from the UV sunlight that certainly caused her hives. She ventured out only at night to place poison pellets in little baskets tied underneath the green shrubbery — a justifiable present for the squirrels who might cause her to fall and break a hip by dropping acorns on her sidewalk. When she was not poisoning squirrels, she called me at work to say that she was going blind.

"You have to come and live with me," she insisted. "I'm an old woman and I can't do anything anymore. I need help with the yard and the house."

I reminded her that I had a daughter to raise and a job to attend. "I live in a different city now, Mama. I have to make a living."

She grew teary, then angry. "You go to see your father more than you come to see me."

"Mama, I see you or Papa every weekend. I haven't had a weekend at home for two years."

"You don't care about me. He has people looking after him night and day. He's living in the Taj Mahal and I'm in this house smothering under all the junk he left here — papers and books and files and records. He abandoned me here, and so did you."

This was not an argument I could win. I cared, but in truth I had always been running away. As a small child she tied bells to my shoelaces to keep track of me as I played in the yard. When I untied the shoes and hung them over a tree branch to blow in the wind, she found out and kept me in my room for the rest of summer. When Papa wandered off in the neighborhood she sent him to a nursing home. My desire to escape her and my preference for my father's company came down to this: He was always leaving — a step ahead of me; she was always following, a hair's breadth behind. I was the sixth horse running toward the outside, stretching my long legs out, sprinting away from the pack, picking up speed, running as fast as I could.

Papa told me that after going to the speedway the nurses had taken him and his roommate Billy Gee to the Rib Shack in Nicholasville for an old soldiers party. "We had one hell of a good time," he said. Maybe, I thought. "And the nurses were dancing in the aisles …"

Maybe, I thought — but not likely.

"And all the waitresses were in the nude …"

Where on earth, I wondered, did Papa's mind go? His stories grew so outrageous that I quit asking the staff about their monthly outings. Finally, I gave up wondering if Papa really went to the races, or to the rib shack, or was sneaking out with Billy Gee in the middle of the night, driving one of five cars they'd hidden on the grounds and drinking moonshine.

I hoped the staff had quit wondering about our family, too. Papa had told them I'd been flying over the Rockies in a hot air balloon, that Mama had trotted onto the 20-yard line at the Hilltoppers' homecoming game to kick the winning goal, and that my daughter became an international billiards champ by beating a Chinese player in a game televised from Boots Bar where everyone was dancing on the tables in the nude.

The people in my father's mind seemed to exude more fun than those of us who were actually taking care of him and measuring out his macaroni, or searching under the bed for his pillow, his underwear, or his teeth. I knew his exuberance couldn't last. Sooner or later he'd do something unpredictable, like stab another patient with his plastic fork at lunch.

So it was. The doctor prescribed something that made Papa a little less lively. The next time I visited him, that the sparkle in his eye — crazy as it may have been — was gone. He spent most of the time curled up on the bed and turned away.

I quit telling Mama when I'd visited Papa. I simply drove on Saturdays, forty-eight miles one way to her house and back. Each trip I hauled away a box of Papa's things and took them home to sort and give away. She never noticed the junk diminishing, but the clothes, books, office supplies and files disappeared two boxes at a time. On Sunday, I'd drive forty-two miles to the veterans' center and back again. I never told Mama the things Papa said when I saw him, or where we went when we went driving. Bundled up in his sweatshirt and pants, a heavy coat, his tweed hat and fuzzy slippers, I'd check him out at the nurses' station.

"Where are you going?" the nurses asked.

"Church," I'd said.

"Are we going to church?" my daughter asked.

"Yeah," I'd tell the nurses; then I'd whisper to Papa, "We're going riding. Keep it under your hat." My father smiled, his eyes glittering.

One day I checked him out and we just kept driving along the back roads to the ferry, then we rode it across the river before driving back to Wilmore again. I noticed, as we passed the thoroughbreds behind their fences, that Papa had stopped talking. Was he upset with me for being gone longer than usual? I didn't want to take him back, but the longer we drove, the more it felt as if we were driving an inevitable road toward a hell that neither of us could mention. I almost said, "Well, the jonquils in the snow bank over there look pretty," but that might have sounded like I was trying to convince him of something. So I didn't say it.

He spoke first. "Do you remember that I love you?"

"Of course," I said.

"I don't always remember things," he said. "But that's something I can remember. I can remember that."

I go again to the closet in my apartment where my father's tweed hat now resides. I'm planning to take the rest of his clothes to the homeless shelter, and I think of the irony of it. For some, homelessness is an earthly reality. For people like my father and me, it's a state of mind. I take down the hat and, closing my eyes, I inhale the dark scent of dust and his long absence. The memories float back, yet still he slips away.

When it comes right down to it, dust is all we are left with. Lying in bed at night I can feel it drift down from the ceiling and cover my eyes with all the finality of the last dirt clod flung. I feel the grit when I wake, as I practically unglue my eyelids, lose an eyelash, and shuffle downstairs to wash my face. In the mirror the lines don't seem to rub off of faces, except on the faces of those we love when we go back into memory. I think of the sweet cracked face of my grandmother, and the wrinkles around Papa's laughing eyes.

One night when no one is watching Papa will fly off like a big-ass bird, singing "Wooo-heee!" He'll lay back his head, jut out his neck and soar like a heron over the creek, dipping into cool water, then up and up. Without any effort the man I call my father will disappear into the light. I'll find him lying in bed, looking up, empty as a blue sky with his mind flown off like a phoenix. With his last blazing thoughts he'll set little brush fires everywhere. He'll roll over onto his back and lift straight up into the sky, singing "Wooo-heee!" — a white spirit, an old man shedding clothes.

MAYTAG

Connie Dean folded a washcloth over her forehead then reached for the beer can sweating on the edge of the bath tub. She enjoyed a beer now and again, especially when her mother visited. Maybelle Flood had been visiting for two months now. When she heard Harold Dean had run off with a shipping clerk from the auto parts store, she begged Connie to come home.

"Honey, I can't do a thing to help you out there in Idaho."

"Don't come," Connie had said, but Maybelle had come.

"I knew you needed me," she said. "And I wouldn't be here if I hadn't known I was needed. I don't know how I made it through that Wyoming road construction in the middle of the night, going seventy miles an hour with my bad cataracts!"

Connie bit her lips and shook her head. "You could have killed somebody!"

Maybelle pulled a long face. "I did it for you, honey, because I love you."

Connie dipped the wash cloth in hot water and folded it over her eyes. After Harold ran off, she wasn't able to come up with the rent, so she'd sold the furniture and moved to Idaho, figuring no bill collector, no husband, no one in his right mind would look for her in Idaho. She listened to her mother banging doors through the nearly empty house. In the next room the television blared a soap opera Maybelle had abandoned watching.

Connie scooped the beer can from the edge of the tub.

Maybelle came blasting through the bathroom door. "You got any towels, underwear, sheets, or things you want washed? We've got to get this laundry done To-day! Connie, you best rise up out of that tub and get yourself down to the Maytag place. See if that man hasn't got any reconditioned washers and dryers...."

"We were just there yesterday."

"You've got to have a washer and dryer. I can't go home 'til you do. Honey, I can't leave you all alone up here with now washer and dryer. You got no husband to help you, and frankly, that daughter of his is the laziest cuss I ever did see."

Maybelle Flood began picking up clothes, grunting, backing her wide bottom into the sink, turning, banging the door with her butt, shifting, and knocking the roll of toilet paper off the wall dispenser. It landed in the toilet and swelled up. In her youth Maybelle had been petite, but as she'd grown older, she'd spread; she'd never gotten used to being wide.

"Mother, please! I'm naked, I'm wet, and I'm taking a bath."

"My mistake." Maybelle glanced into the mirror to arrange the look of hurt on her face.

She pulled the last towel from the towel rack and opened the door, her arms overflowing with dirty clothes, bathrobes, and towels. On her way out, she banged her right hip into the wall, then her left hip into the doorway. She dropped a pair of Connie's underwear into the toilet; they sat floating on top of the toilet paper. Maybelle left the door ajar and Connie watched her waddle down the carpeted hall, a woman with a mission. As she passed, Maybelle bellowed into her granddaughter's room, "Heloise, you got any ..."

Heloise slammed her bedroom door and turned up her Sesame Street tape player.

Connie rose from the tub, dripping onto the floor, and shut the door. Twice she searched the bathroom for a towel, but Maybelle had taken the last one — Connie's bathrobe, too, and the clean clothes as well as the dirty. "Shit," Connie muttered and stalked into the hall. Naked, she stood before the linen closet, searching for a clean towel.

"Why, Connie!" her mother said, coming back down the hall. "You shouldn't be out here all exposed like that. The neighbors can see right through those open windows. And don't think they won't either. You got to get yourself some shades ... Honey, you're dripping all over the carpet!"

Reaching for the towel farthest back in the linen closet, Connie mouthed a scream.

Connie, Maybelle, and Heloise stood beside the dusty car outside Bud's Suds 'n' Duds watching a mechanized washer woman, her hair tied Aunt Jemima fashion, raise and lower herself over an old washboard and tub.

"Look at that, Heloise!" exclaimed Maybelle. "You know, my mother — your great grandmother, used to wash her clothes like that...."

Heloise threw her hands over her ears. "I know you done told me a hundred thousand times!"

"Heloise!" hissed Connie. "Don't be ugly."

She opened the back door of the pebble-pocked car. Maybelle moved in quickly, her wide hips knocking Connie out of the way. She grunted as she heaved the mountain of clothes in the laundry basket. The basket was plastic and not heavy, but Maybelle made animal noises which indicated how hard she was working.

"Uh, uh, uh," she grunted.

"Mom, let me do that."

"You got enough to do already. Heloise, grab me that laundry soap."

"You get it," said Heloise, slamming the car door.

Connie scooped up the softener and soap.

Inside Buds Suds 'n' Duds, Heloise found a dirty corner of the floor and sat with her back to her mother and grandmother. She played alone with her Ken and Barbie dolls. Barbie's yellow hair had been whacked off with a pair of child-safe scissors and Ken's face bore the tattoos of black and green magic markers.

"I can't go on like this," sighed Barbie.

"Let's you and me blow this dump," said Ken.

Heloise marched her dolls up and down the floor, humming bridal music. Maybelle tumbled the laundry into a pile on the folding table and began sorting, reading labels, and turning clothes right side out. Connie wished her mother wouldn't sort through her threadbare undergarments, her soiled towels, her stained and sweaty blouses.

"Uh, uh, uh," Maybelle grunted happily.

"I'll do that," Connie said. "You go sit."

"Oh, you won't let me help you at all. Honey, I just want to help you. That's all I ever wanted. I just ..."

"It's okay, Mom. Just sit down. It's fine."

She snatched up a pile of clothes and dropped them into heaps of light and dark. When she finished she wiped her hands and shoved five dollar bills into a change machine. Quarters rumbled through the machine then clanked into the receiving slot.

"Marry me, honey pie," said Ken. "And give me a TV kiss!"

"Eek!" shrieked Barbie and ran away with him.

Heloise looked up from her dolls. "I want pop," she said.

"A soda?"

"Pop."

"She wants a coke," said Maybelle.

Connie gave Heloise two quarters for the soft drink machine.

"All that sugar," said Maybelle to no one in particular.

Connie shoved quarters into six washing machines sitting side by side. As the water tumbled into the wash bins, the sleepy laundromat stirred to life. She measured cups of soap; the bins frothed with crackling bubbles. She dropped her clothes into the suds until over her shoulder she saw Maybelle coming along behind her, pulling out underwear and scrubbing them with a Wisk-soaked toothbrush.

"That's not necessary," Connie said. "These old clothes don't come clean."

"Wait and see," said Maybelle. "I've done laundry before."

Connie stared through the dusty Laundromat windows. The steam streaming inside did nothing to remove the dirt caked on the outside. She bought herself a soda and sank into a folding chair. Heloise, in the corner, slurped her soft drink, while Maybelle settled into a chair and began snapping and organizing a copy of yesterday's newspaper. Connie listened to the sound of her clothes turning clean.

She'd first discovered that Harold had run off when she'd gone to work at the beauty parlor, same as usual. As she snapped on her smock, her best friend, Suzanne, the next chair over, rushed up breathlessly to say, "I tell you, Connie, I went into total shock this morning when I heard Harold left you for that tramp!"

"Harold left me?" asked Connie. She wondered absently whether she should leave the thawed chicken in the refrigerator and bring home Chinese food that night.

"Yeah, I know, honey." Suzanne shook her Medusa curls. "And I feel just awful about it. But I tell you what, when that little bitch came in here saying how she was leaving town with her soul mate — your Harold Dean, Connie — and she wanted a brand new 'do. Well, she sat in my chair …"

"Harold's her soul mate?"

"Yeah, the little hussy, but I got her for you. Lemme tell you what I did. You're my best friend, Connie — I did it for you. I frizzed the bitch's head."

Connie heard the wash cycle stop. The machines clunked, changing gears, then the rinse cycle began to spray. The water told her to be quiet, not to think; it said, "Sshhhhhhhh!"

"Now, here's a washer and dryer for two-hundred-ninety-five dollars!" said Maybelle, snapping the paper. "There's another for one fifty." She frowned and sucked something out of her teeth. "Bet it's no good." She read on, and then stopped. "Now! Here's the one …"

Maybelle began pulling out Kleenex and gum, things from the depths of her immense black purse until she found some scissors, a pencil and the back of an envelope. "Uh, uh," she grunted, sucked the pencil, and wrote: W/Ds. Then she snipped items from the classified ads and filed them.

Heloise smacked her dolls' heads together. They were either kissing or fighting.

"'Til death do us part," said Ken.

"Ackk!" said Barbie.

Heloise threw her dolls in the corner. "I want Pop," she said.

"You just had a pop," said Connie.

"No, I mean my Pop. I want to go home. He's probably waiting for us. It's been years already! He told me I could have a kitty."

"When did he say that?"

"I don't know. He was mowing the lawn. He said, 'Last goddamn time I do this,' then he kissed me on the head and said I could have a kitty."

"I thought Harold was allergic to cats," said Maybelle, snipping.

"Listen, Heloise, if you want a cat, we can get a cat, but we're home already. We live in Idaho. You understand?"

"I don't think you should have a cat in the house," said Maybelle. "They spray."

"I want a kitty," said Heloise. "*And* I want Pop."

"Heloise, your Pop doesn't live with us any more."

"No sir, I wouldn't have any cats. They leave hair all over and tear up the furniture."

"Mother!" Connie shouted.

Maybelle hushed, grunted three times, and kept snipping. Heloise gave Maybelle a sour look over Connie's shoulder. "Meow," she said, and then whispered, "When's grandma going home?"

Connie frowned. "Heloise, be nice."

When the spin cycle stopped, Connie gave Heloise two quarters for another pop. She emptied the clean clothes into three dryers and shoved in a few quarters. Finished clipping, Maybelle tucked the envelope in her purse along with the folded, shredded newspaper.

Connie stood before the dryer watching the clothes tumble. The sleeves of her blue blouse clutched the legs of Maybelle's black polyester slacks. Heloise's green socks kicked Connie's blue jeans in the butt. Generations of clothes chased each other around in the dryer, making contact, sliding away. When she returned to her seat she found Heloise curled up asleep, her head in her grandmother's lap. Maybelle's puffy fingers stroked the child's sticky, sweating cheek.

"Sweet," Maybelle said.

Connie nodded.

"Look at her — those little eyelashes and that tiny mouth. She looks just like you. Just like my baby."

Connie knew the minute she turned the corner that she shouldn't have gone down Broadway. The clothes were folded in neat piles ready to be put away. Maybelle, reading the paper, was consumed with thoughts of politics and other things she couldn't fix. Heloise, asleep in the passenger's seat, probably would have stayed that way until dinner. Everything was all right, and then Connie turned the wrong corner.

"There's the Maytag place!" cried Maybelle, squirming between the stacks of laundry. "Stop right here. Right now, Connie, before they close!" Maybelle scratched around the inside of the car, trying to find the door handle.

"Mom, let's just go home."

"We're right here! It'll only take a minute."

Connie parked and Maybelle scrambled out of the car, tugged the stretched blouse over her stomach, and patted her poofy white hairdo once. Her sharp yellow teeth snapped together into a frightening smile. Ominous as thunder the old woman blew through the door. Connie heard the dusty cow bell clang above the door. An empty grocery sack buffeted down the street. She looked at Heloise asleep — Barbie in her lap, Ken had rolled onto the floor somewhere. She sighed, locked her child in the car, and followed Maybelle into the store. Connie smiled, about to speak, then faltered. The door banged shut and spanked her.

Maybelle spoke first. She stood before the clerk's battered wooden desk and raised four puffy fingers. "I've been here FOUR times — FOUR times! — and I've had no satisfaction. No ma'am, no satisfaction. I want to know about that washer and dryer To-Day!"

Connie blanched and turned toward the window, fingering the price tag on an avocado washing machine beside her and trying to keep an eye on Heloise. She watched the wind scour sand and dry leaves down the street.

The sales clerk glanced from one woman to the other, her eyes sliding in and out of focus. "I'm sorry. Who did you say you were?"

"Maybelle Flood! You got my name and number!" She rolled her eyes across the shiny row of washers, dryers, and microwave ovens. "This IS Jim Dandy's Maytag, isn't it? That Mr. Dandy of yours said he'd sell me a reconditioned washer and dryer To-day!"

The clerk pressed her lips together and tutted. "Why, honey, there's no Mr. Dandy here. That's just the store name."

"Well, it was some man!" snapped Maybelle. "Whatever man works here." Her eyes flickered like far-off lightning. "I got his name here somewhere."

She heaved her oversized black purse onto the counter, puffed out her cheeks, blew her thick, white bangs over her forehead, and sighed. Maybelle began tugging bundles from her purse, snapping rubber bands, shuffling papers — scraps of envelopes with names and phone numbers, store coupons, grocery lists, cancelled checks, newspaper clippings, pictures of Heloise, assorted throat lozenges, and peanuts, sticks of gum, and give-away fast food chain restaurant toothpicks — everything individually wrapped in sealed plastic Handiwraps and secured with more rubber bands. She dumped the items onto the counter.

"Wait here," said the sales clerk and left.

"Mother," Connie whispered hoarsely. "Please don't."

Maybelle turned toward Connie, raised her penciled eyebrow and gave a wink. "Oh, you'll get your Maytag, all right. Mark my words. The squeaky wheel gets the grease."

The first clerk returned with a second who wore a pasted-on smile. She approached Maybelle with her hands composed at her waist. "We close in five, but maybe I can help you a minute. Which washer and dryer were you looking at?"

The first clerk sat at her desk and hid her frown behind a stack of paperwork. Now and again she peeked around the paper's edge at Maybelle.

"Whichever Maytag that man was going to sell me for two hundred dollars. I haven't seen it yet. I never buy anything I don't see. That's why we're here." She swept her arm across the room indicating Connie. "That's my daughter, Connie Dean. I'm buying the washer and dryer for her."

Connie leaned further into the display case window, but she still couldn't see around the corner to her car. She hoped Heloise was asleep. She bit her lips and pressed her cheek into the dusty glass window.

The clerk eyed her and smiled as if she had a gas pain, which then released her and the smile faded. "We never recondition Maytags. We sometimes have Hotpoints, GEs, and Kenmores waiting to be fixed, but I don't know when that will be. Just leave your name with Shirley here. She'll give you a call tomorrow. Thanks for stopping by."

Connie stirred to life. "That's fine. Call us. Come on, Mom. Let's go."

"I need that washer and dryer To-day!" sniffed Maybelle. "That man said he'd have me a washer and dryer within a day or two. It's been a month now. I'm getting no satisfaction. No satisfaction."

"What man?" the clerk asked.

Maybelle scratched through the contents of her purse which were now spread out across the counter. She lifted small scraps of paper and examined them. She looked in her empty purse, then back at the counter. "I wrote his name down on one of these cards here. Just gimme a minute to find it."

The first clerk cleared her throat and shook her head quickly. The second clerk watched all the proceedings from the corner of her eye.

"Oh well, it could be anybody," she said. "We got eight repairmen. Ed, Alan, Shep ..."

"And not a one of them can fix a washer and dryer, I assume."

The clerk's thin grey lips snapped together like two pieces of flint. She glanced upward, watching an indolent moth on the ceiling. "You can leave your name and number and check with us later."

"I did check with you later. Today is later. I've been here four times. My name is Maybelle Flood and you've got my name and number."

Connie heard a noise in the street. She thought she heard a car door slam. She rushed toward Maybelle and tugged at her sweater. "Let's go, Mom. They're closing in five. Thank you so much," she told the clerk. "We'll check back later." She tugged Maybelle's sleeve. The sweater stretched, but Maybelle stayed solid within it.

"Stop tugging on me, Connie Dean. Do you want a washer and dryer or not?"

"Thanks so much. We'll come back. Goodbye."

"Connie Dean, what the hell's the matter with you?"

"C'mon Mom. I can't leave Heloise asleep in the car."

The clerk grimaced a final time. "Thanks for stopping by!" she said loudly. As if on cue, the first clerk appeared with a clipboard full of inventory papers. The second glanced through the list, mumbled "uh-hmmm, uh-hmmm," then both disappeared through the inner door. In the back office a file drawer slammed; the light switched off.

Maybelle pinched her fingers in the air. "We were about that close to getting a washer and dryer, and now look what you've done. If I left it up to you, you never would get a washer and dryer."

Connie let go of her mother's sweater. "It doesn't matter. They're closing. Let's go. Heloise is out in the car." She headed for the door.

Maybelle stood a moment beneath a twirling red and yellow sign that read "Our Biggest Sale Ever!" She peered through the doorway after the women, rewrapped her papers, replaced all the rubber bands with a snap, snap, snap, layered the papers in her purse, snapped its brass clasp and waited. The dusty bell tinkled. She glanced backward to see Connie Dean holding open the door with her hip.

"You coming?"

Out on the sidewalk Maybelle patted her hair again and shook her head. "Can you imagine! I don't guess they sell many appliances with sales people like that."

Heloise stood on the sidewalk crying, the car door open. She clutched Barbie tightly. "Mom, Ken's gone! I lost my Ken! We got to go back and get him!"

"Get in the car, Heloise," Connie growled. "C'mon, Mom. Let's go."

Connie hopped behind the wheel and waited for Maybelle to climb over the curb, open her door, and scrunch in between the laundry. When the door creaked shut Connie stepped on the gas.

Connie dreamed she died and lay on a bier of lilies while another Connie watched. Then the real Connie accidentally slipped into a deep hole in the ground. When she looked up, she saw daylight a long way off and Maybelle, Heloise, and Harold peering down into the hole. Connie struggled to get up, but the dirt was sandy and soft. She kept digging herself in deeper. "Quit foolin' around," Maybelle said. "We're gonna be late for the funeral."

She woke to the rumble of thunder — no, it was just Maybelle snoring in the back room. Heloise slept on a mattress on the floor beside Connie, amid an orgy of Little Ponies, Barbies and Mitzies. Holding her breath, Connie slipped over Heloise and tiptoed into the living room. She stared at the cardboard boxes sitting where she had dumped them two months ago. The uncurtained windows yawned like dark mouths. She thought she'd labeled everything before she left, but the box in front of her only said: Stuff. In it were bills she hadn't paid, coffee mugs, clean towels, and a pair of candles now fused with their candlesticks. The dust had become part of the wax. Connie and Harold used to eat dinner by candlelight until he accused her of using the half-dark to hide her burnt meatloaf.

Then she found a shoe box of creased and ragged photographs with pictures of Connie and Harold at the ball game where they first met, pictures of their wedding, pictures of Heloise, just born, sitting between them. As the years grew more recent Connie and Harold had stood farther apart, until they no longer appeared in the same picture.

"Mom!" Heloise shouted from the hall.

Connie jumped and threw the lid over the shoe box. Heloise rubbed her eyes with the back of one hand which held three Barbies by their ponytails. Their oversized plastic breasts jabbed into her cheekbone.

"Is it time for school?"

"No, honey. Still night. Go back to bed."

"I can't," whined Heloise. "I'm lonely."

Connie stretched out her arms to her daughter, and Heloise and the three Barbies climbed into her lap. Heloise took the lid off the shoe box and looked at the pictures. She stared a long time at the photo of Harold kissing her on her first Christmas.

"Miss your Poppy?"

Heloise looked up. It was a trick question and Connie wished she hadn't asked.

"Can I still have a kitty?"

"Hard to say."

"Is he coming back?"

"Hard to say," Connie repeated and yawned as if by mistake. It was three in the morning. She and Heloise were sitting in their flannel night gowns in a nearly empty house in a brightly lit, vacant room with no curtains at the windows. "Jeez, it's getting late. We ought to be in bed."

Heloise stalled, picked up another photo and bent over it looking. There was Maybelle with Heloise when Heloise was three. Just as the picture snapped, Heloise had decided to jump up and Maybelle was snatching the fleeing child's nightshirt.

"How come she's always grabbing on us?" asked Heloise.

"I don't know. Come on, honey. Let's go to bed. We can unpack the rest of these in the afternoon when we get home."

After Connie and Heloise threw backward kisses over their shoulders and left, and after the dishes were done, Maybelle pulled out her envelope of clippings. She sat by the telephone arranging the ads into piles, then began dialing.

"Hello. About your washer and dryer ... Oh well, you sold it already. I see. Thank you very much ... Hello. About that ad for a washer and dryer ... Well, what do you mean the washer needs work? I see. All right. Thank you very much ... Hello. About your washer. What kind is it? Mmm-hmm. And do you have a dryer? You don't? I see. Well, let me give you my name and number...."

She marked X's and O's across her list and kept dialing.

"Hello …"

"Jim Dandy's Maytag."

"Pardon?"

"Jim Dandy's Maytag."

Maybelle hung up, twiddled her pencil a minute, then dialed again.

"Jim Dandy's Maytag."

"Good morning," she said, coiling a lock of hair around her finger. "My name is Connie Dean, and I'm looking for a good reconditioned washer and dryer. I notice you have a set for $200. What kind is it? … A Maytag? Oh Really? Could I come by and see it? … Tomorrow. Well, why can't I come today? … I see, you have someone else looking at it. Well, why don't I give you my name and number…"

After she hung up, Maybelle dressed quickly, styled her poofy white hair, and drove to Jim Dandy's Maytag Store. Out on the sidewalk she stretched her sweater over her protruding stomach, hooked the black purse over her arm, and palmed the newspaper clipping in her hand. When her armor was ready, she heaved open the door. The cow bell went bang! against the glass. She held up her fingers to the clerk.

"Fifth time!" she said.

The clerk opened her eyes wide, and then ducked into the inner office. Maybelle waited. She glanced around the store at the new Maytags. "Dusty," she said. She lifted the corner of a red sale tag sticker and found the price was exactly the same. This time the clerk returned with an older, beefy man. He tugged his brown, pilled sweater over his belly and pulled a cigarette out of his mouth. The cigarette fumed behind him in his cupped hand.

"Help you?"

"You're the man I came to see. Are you Mr. Dandy?"

"Yeah, sure. What can I do for you?"

"I want to see that reconditioned Maytag washer and dryer."

"Don't have one. Leave your number with Shirley here, and we'll get back to you. He turned, flicked his ash, and headed for the office.

"Pardon me, but when I called, this lady said you did have a used washer and dryer someone was looking at. Well, I want to see it."

He threw an ugly snarl at the clerk. "Sorry. We sold it this morning."

"Is that so? I called no more than five minutes ago."

"Look, lady, we don't have one. What's your point?"

"The point is I've been here five times to buy a washer and dryer ..."

"We got plenty. Have a look."

"Used," Maybelle said. She waved the classified in his face. "Just like this ad says. You advertised something, Mr. Dandy, that you haven't got."

He drew on his cigarette and exhaled in Maybelle's face. The ashes collapsed onto his sweater and he patted them into its threads. "So?"

Maybelle puffed her bangs and blew his smoke back at him. "It's false advertising. I could have you arrested," she sniffed.

"I told you," complained the clerk. "You can't keep expecting people to come back and finally buy a new washing machine."

"Shut up, Shirley," he said. "You're fired."

"Fired, my ass! I quit." She snatched her purse and sweater from a peg and stormed out the door. The cow bell banged so hard it cracked the glass and fell to the floor.

"So there!" said Maybelle and stormed out after her. Then she stood on the sidewalk, her mouth blowing a tornado, telling anyone who walked by what happened inside Jim Dandy's Maytag — what she had said, what he had said, and what the clerk did. Then it occurred to her that Connie still didn't have a washer and dryer. She drove home and started calling other listings in her envelope, leaving her name and number. That afternoon in the middle of The Love Connection, the telephone rang.

"Hot diggity!" shouted Maybelle. "We got ourselves a washer and dryer!" She cleared her throat and smoothed her blouse to answer the telephone. "Good afternoon."

"Connie, is that you? Listen, honey, we got to talk ... Connie? Connie, don't hang up on me. Connie?"

Maybelle jerked the phone out of its wall socket.

When Connie and Heloise came home at 3:30 Jeopardy was blaring out of the television, while Maybelle snored on the couch. She'd been busy. Wrinkled curtains hung at the windows, airing. Piles of crumpled newspapers, cardboard boxes and assorted things Connie hadn't seen in months littered the floor — more Barbie dolls, a Ken, books, kitchen spices, stationery, cleaning supplies. Pictures Connie had forgotten she owned hung on the walls; ugly ceramic knick-knacks marred the bookshelves.

"My Ken!" shouted Heloise, tossing her school satchel into a pile of boxes and crumpled newspapers. She snatched up the doll and hugged him. "Oh, honey! Where ya been?"

Ken ran with Heloise into the bedroom to reunite with his harem of Barbies. Connie stared at the boxes marked Junk — piles of men's clothes, photographs of Harold, a box of feathers he and Heloise had found on the mesas of New Mexico.

"Honeys! I'm home," shouted Ken. "Where's my dinner?"

"So what do you think?" asked Maybelle, yawning. She looked like a tornado at rest.

"I need a beer," said Connie, heading toward the kitchen. "What's the phone doing unplugged?" She pushed the connector into the wall. It rang.

"Hello?"

"Why'd you hang up on me like that?"

"Who is this?"

"Wha'da ya mean? It's Harold."

Connie hung up and glared at her mother. "Now, I really need that beer." She swung open the refrigerator and stuck her head inside. The cold air smacked her face. There was only an opened Diet Pepsi with its fizz gone. "You should have told me Harold called."

"Oh yeah. He called. I hung up on him for you."

"For me?"

"Yeah. Don't the house look nice?" asked Maybelle, yawning and stretching again. "I'm plumb tuckered out. I've been busy all day. Looks just like home, don't you think?"

It looked like Maybelle's home. If Connie didn't watch it, it would start filling up with furniture wrapped in plastic. The phone rang again.

"Don't answer it," said Maybelle. "I'll get it. I'll pretend you're not here. No, I'll pretend it's a wrong number."

"He knows it's not. We've hung up on him twice."

"I'll tell him you're in the shower."

"Smart," said Connie. "Why don't I just move to Canada?"

The phone rang. Maybelle reached for it.

"I'll get it," said Connie. "It's my phone ... Hello?"

"Maybelle Flood!" shouted the man on the other end. "If you dare bring your fat face in my store again, if you ever slander me out on the sidewalk in front of my store again, I'll sue your ass. I'll ..."

"Wrong number," Connie said and hung up. She tipped up the Pepsi as if it were a Budweiser. "So, what did you do all day, Mom?"

"Oh, a little of this, a little of that. Organizing, you know."

"Go anywhere?"

Maybelle sniffed, smelling a trap. "Well, now, I did. And, Connie, it's a good thing I went, too. That place doesn't sell a thing but brand new Maytags ..."

"And you made a scene on the sidewalk."

"I did not make a scene! You know your mother. I just got firm and spoke my mind ... Now, I believe I did find you a washer and dryer, a Kenmore. Course, it's $275, but we'll talk her down. Wait and see if we don't."

One at a time Heloise threw her Mitzy dolls into the hallway. "Now, get out and stay out," shouted the Barbies in unison.

"I haven't seen them yet. They're out in one of those little towns near here. Naphtha, I think."

"Nampa."

"We got to drive out there tonight and look at it. We got to get you a washer and dryer in here. I can't keep running back and forth to the Laundromat."

"You can't. Then you're staying?" asked Connie. The phone rang. "Jesus! What is it with this phone? ... HELLO!"

"Connie, don't hang up on me, goddamn it. You're still married to me."

"What do you want, Harold?"

"Lemme see Heloise. I got rights to see Heloise."

"You left. You told her you weren't coming back."

Heloise ran into the hall with the five Barbies. They kissed Ken and carried him back down the hall into Heloise's room, cooing, "Oh, little sweetie!"

"Don't get bitchy with me, Connie! What the hell's a matter with you?"

"Buzz off, Harold! I don't want to talk right now."

"You talk to me, Connie! You talk to me now!"

She hung up. Maybelle tutted and patted her poofy hair.

"See now, that's why I unplugged the phone. I did it for you, honey."

The phone rang. "My god, it's a national telethon." Connie picked it up. "Harold, I don't want to talk right now ..."

"Excuse me. Hello, excuse me. Is this 355-8392?"

"Oh, sorry," said Connie. "Yes, it is."

"I've got that Kenmore here. I been waiting all afternoon for you to look at it. You come right now 'cause I've got to leave in about an hour."

"What Kenmore?"

"Ain't you the lady what called me about my Kenmore?"

"No, I ain't," said Connie. "I don't want your damned Kenmore!"

She hung up. Maybelle fumed.

"You'll be sorry now. It took me two months to find that washer and dryer."

"Arrgh!" screamed Connie. "I don't want a washer and dryer. I never said I wanted a washer and dryer. You just decided I needed one. The way you decided to drive out here when I told you not to come. The way you decided I'm not supposed to talk to Harold. The way ..."

"My mistake," Maybelle sniffed.

"Maybe I don't like knick-knacks on my shelves. Maybe I'd rather not have curtains at the window."

"You got to have curtains, Connie Dean!"

"Why didn't you ask me? Nobody ever asks me."

"I was just trying to help. Tell me what you want done and I'll do it."

"That's not the point," Connie said.

The phone rang. Maybelle reached for it.

Connie laid her hand over the phone. "I think it's time for you to go home now."

Maybelle's eyes flashed. She patted her poofy white hair and uplifted her chin. Connie steadied her gaze, her hand on the phone. The fluorescent light over the sink buzzed. The phone rang again.

"Mom, I'm hungry," said Heloise. "What's for dinner?"

The phone rang again.

"I don't know," Connie said.

"Aren't you going to answer it?" asked Maybelle.

"What's for dinner?" asked Heloise.

"I'm trying to decide," said Connie.

The phone rang again.

"I'm hungry now," moaned Heloise.

The phone rang and rang and rang and rang, then it stopped.

Maybelle sat in the kitchen, her packed bags on the sofa. The sun had just crested in the east and flashed a peach-colored light onto the sandy hills north of town. She cleaned out her purse, dumping coupons, old envelopes, lists, and clippings. A light rain the night before had cleaned off the car and settled the dust on the road.

She sighed. "I've been gone so long. I bet my house is a mess. I'll be dusting for a week."

Connie woke Heloise. The three of them sat in the kitchen eating bran muffins, drinking milk and coffee, then Connie carried the fat brown bags to her mother's car. Maybelle patted her hair once and got behind the wheel.

"No driving at night," Connie said. "And keep it under seventy."

"I love you, honey. More than anything in the world, I just wish I could ..." She stopped herself.

"I know."

"You going to be all right?"

"Fine," said Connie. "Heloise and I will be just fine." She hugged her daughter tight. Heloise backed away a little, inspecting her mother.

"Okay, then." Maybelle cranked the key again, grinding the motor. She blushed, blinked back the tears and shook her head. "Bye-bye!" She mouthed the words again, bye-bye. Maybelle pulled slowly away from the drive and waved into the rear view mirror.

Ken and Barbie waved back.

"Where's grandma going?" asked Heloise.

"Home."

"Is she coming back?"

"Oh, I expect so." Connie stopped waving and steered her daughter into the house. "In a year or so. I doubt we could stop her if we tried."

ACTING LESSONS

For Mama's seventieth birthday Papa planned a surprise party. It wasn't so much a birthday party as it was a debut. Her part in "Sweet Bird of Youth" represented a long-delayed spotlight she'd dreamed about for fifty-five years. She'd given herself a stage name, and had taken to answering the phone that way when anybody called.

A week before the play opened, I called our house to talk to Mama, but the person who answered the phone didn't sound at all like my mother. Instead, she had a vaguely familiar, but entirely sultry Southern voice. She answered my tentative inquiry by saying, "No, your mother is not here. This is Belle Fitzgerald. I could take a message for her…."

I could hear the little smirk in her voice, so I played along.

"Well, if you don't mind…" I said, "I'm sure Mama won't be in a cooking mood on opening night. I'm planning to take her and Papa to dinner on Thursday a week from now. Could you let her know?"

"Honey," she said in her Mama's voice. "You don't have to take me to dinner. I'll just fix some left-over spaghetti or something."

"No," I insisted. "I want to do it."

Actually I wanted to get her out of the house. Papa had sneaked downstairs and called me at work a few minutes before from the phone in my basement apartment. That's when we'd arranged the ruse.

"It's the least I can do for a soon-to-be famous actress," I said.

ACTING LESSONS

It was 'just a little bitty old part,' as Mama put it. She only came on in the second act, but it was impossible not to notice how, as she bustled around the house, she whispered her lines in a breathy voice. "Chance. Chance ... You come out here ... I can't be seen talking to you...."

"Mama," I suggested, "don't you think that voice is a bit too sultry for Aunt Nonnie?"

Mama looked shocked. "What do you mean? I was just trying to keep it down so as not to disturb your father's television watching."

The play was being produced by the Every Now and Then Theatre, so-called because every now and then somebody in town got bored, then decided to do a play. Whether anybody else wanted to see it was another question. When auditions were announced in the paper, Mama latched onto it as a kind of self-improvement project — which was fine with me. At least it was herself she wanted to improve instead of me, my daughter Helene, or Papa.

The director was an acquaintance of mine, a recently graying man who'd pierced his nose and dyed his hair green before it became fashionable among high school kids. Because he lived alone, he peopled his living room with cross-dressed mannequins, composed of severed and impossibly re-attached body parts. Sherman Bass was harmless enough, but the hedgehog he kept as a pet would shit all over his kitchen. When Mama said she needed to pick up the script from him, I offered to do it, saying I had to go out anyway. I was afraid she'd get upset and quit before the play ever got started.

Not that Mama hadn't had adventures in her day. I'm sure she had. For a time when she'd lived in San Francisco, she'd been a chorus line dancer in the U.S.O. Papa still kept in his wallet a picture of her and the other bathing beauties taken by the ocean on one of the piers. With her long, curly auburn hair, Mama looked just like Vivien Leigh.

In the week before the play opened, Papa'd taken to sneaking into the basement to phone up Mama's relatives and announce her debut. He must have invited fifty people to the party. While Mama was at rehearsal, I cleaned her house so she wouldn't be embarrassed when her many fans showed up.

Mama and I began buying groceries at different stores all over town, so that she could drive and practice her lines, while I held the book. "Oh Chance, why have you changed like you've changed? Why do you live on nothing but wild dreams now ... Oh, it's sad," Mama said, interrupting herself. "See, he just took one of those pills the Princess Kosmonopolis has gotten him hooked on. He's not a bad boy; he's just made a few mistakes, but haven't we all? Boss is this evil man, and Chance is madly in love with Heavenly, that's Boss's daughter ..." For a moment, it seemed she'd stepped into one of the soap operas she usually occupied herself with in the afternoons. Only a loudly honking car dragged her out of reverie. She scowled at the other driver.

"What's he honking at me for?"

"That was a stop sign, Mama."

"Oh."

Along the way, she bustled out of the car with arms full of posters that Sherman had asked the cast to pitch in and have printed; then he'd asked everyone to distribute them. On a crusade for art, Mama tried to see if she could plaster more paper on more store fronts in town than anybody else. "This town needs some culture. It always has," she said, taping a poster to the Chinese restaurant window. "It doesn't matter to me if anyone knows I'm in the play or not." She pointed to the poster. "See, there I am."

"Mama," I protested. "You didn't put your name on it."

"Yes, I did. That's my stage name. I never liked my real name. I never liked that woman at all. I'm Belle Fitzgerald now."

In the evenings, I re-heated supper, usually whatever leftovers Mama took out of the freezer and thawed that afternoon. While she wrestled first one thigh, then the other into her girdle, I heard her in the bedroom reciting lines, punctuated by the sound of snapping rubber. "You come out here ... (snap) You come out here ... (snap) You come out here ..." Her bedroom sounded crowded with voices, including a coquette, a black woman, and a shrew. Then came a hushed, angry voice I almost recognized. "I can't be seen talking to you ..."

Papa, Helene, and I ate warmed-over chili and crackers on trays in front of the television. Mama emerged from the bedroom looking stellar, even at nearly seventy, wearing gold earrings, brick red lipstick, and a tawny brushed cotton dress with a leopard spotted scarf. Papa stared open-mouthed and fish-eyed like he didn't know whether he should buy her a drink or take her home to his mother.

"Do I look all right?" Mama asked.

"Yeah," Papa said. He sounded like he was going to cry.

Helene glanced at her grandmother, then turned her back to watch more television. "She thinks she's somebody," Helene muttered.

"I'm having dinner with Mrs. Castigone and Buddy Hopper at Bullfrog's," Mama said. "We're going to study lines before rehearsal. I'll be back about ten or ten-thirty." She gathered her purse and car keys.

"Sounds good," I said. "Have fun."

It was about time Mama started having a life again. She hadn't had much of one since Papa's stroke. It felt a little like she was leaving us in the dust, though. I opened the door for her. Brittle November oak leaves blew through the grass.

"Weather's turned," I said. "You'd better take your coat."

"Don't forget to give your father his medicine at 9:00."

"I won't forget, Mama," I promised, closing the door.

"Grandmother thinks she's a movie star," Helene observed, "but it's just a stupid old play."

"Naw," I said. "She's just having fun."

When Mama returned, she found me sitting in her chair, hemming a pair of pants for Helene. Helene lay crashed out in front of the blaring television in a pile of school papers, her head on her multiplication tables. Papa snored with his glasses above his eyebrows and an unfinished shopping list balled up under his fists. It read: vodka, bourbon, scotch, ice, tonic.

"So how was it?"

"Fine. I knew all my lines. I'm the only one who did."

While she took off her coat, I wandered over to Papa, pretending to remove and fold up his glasses, then sneaked the party list out of his hand, and stuffed it in my bathrobe pocket. In the kitchen I set the kettle on to boil and pulled two cups from the cupboard. Mama pulled the step stool up to the counter.

"I don't think your friend Sherman is very happy with me. I don't think he likes actors. He keeps telling us what to do, saying, 'Move this way,' and 'Louder! I can't hear you.' He says, 'Belle, quit moving your hands when you talk.' Well, you know me. I'm not talking if I'm not moving my hands." She was moving her hands, talking, pointing, and waving her cigarette, then fiddling with her scarf, followed by opening and closing her purse. She was wound up real tight — had been for three straight weeks. "He says, 'Just act natural. Act natural!'"

"Well, that's his job, Mama. He's the director."

She flicked her ashes, waving her cigarette back and forth like she was erasing a child's crayon picture from a wall. "I don't think he likes the way I talk either. He kept saying it was a Southern play, you know, and we were supposed to sound Southern, but tonight he called me phony. He actually cursed me, 'Just say the line, god damn it!' I don't know why he was picking on me. Nobody else sounded Southern ..."

"That's 'cause most of them are from somewhere up North."

"That's it exactly," Mama agreed. "Every night during break I have to teach them how to talk."

I picked up the kettle before it whistled, not wanting to wake everybody in the house. "You don't have to pretend Mama. Just be yourself."

"Well, that's what I'm doing. I'm myself. Haven't I always been precisely myself?" She sipped her tea and fell silent. I patted my chest in search of the needle and thread, then picked up my sewing again.

"As if Belle Fitzgerald wasn't born Southern," she grumbled.

In the morning, while the bacon sizzled untended, Belle cornered Helene by the stove and brandished a hairbrush at her. Helene swatted her hands as if frenzied bees were attacking. "Child, you're in fourth grade now! If you don't have sense enough to act like a young lady, at least you can look like one. No child of mine is going to school with her hair looking like it'd been run through a Mix-Master."

I interrupted. "Mama, that's my child." I took the hairbrush and handed her the pronged fork to turn the bacon. The kitchen smelled oily. "Come here, Helene. Don't piss off your grandmother first thing in the morning. It's not polite. She might not feed you."

"I never had a new dress one, when I was your age," Mama scolded. "I stuffed newspapers inside my sister's shoes so they'd fit. I was poor, but I never went to school looking like it. I brushed my hair 100 strokes every morning. When I went out I held my head high, like it had a crown on it, like I was somebody. And I was. I was somebody the Good Lord cared enough to die for ..." For Mama, it was a short walk from a topic like hair brushing to salvation. I knew I needed to hush her, but Helene beat me to it.

"Somebody pretending she's somebody doesn't make her anybody."

That stopped her. Mama fish-breathed a minute, opening and closing her mouth, then she shook her head like a dog shaking off water. "You could stand a few acting lessons from your grandmother."

Helene stormed out of the kitchen, shouting at the wind behind her. "You'll be sorry you were mean to me when I'm more famous than you." Mama peered after her until she'd disappeared around the corner.

"Well," Belle said, "the kid's got ambition."

That afternoon Mama ran lines with Helene in the back seat while I drove them around town, delivering posters, stopping wherever Mama wanted to shop for new dresses. Helene did everything she could to irritate me, including standing frozen in the glass front store windows pretending to be one of the mannequins, or stealing umbrellas from their stands and wandering the store tap-tapping and turning her head as if she were blind. Strangers looked at me with pity. For some reason Mama decided to dress up Helene for opening night. Every dress she brought to Helene, I had to coerce her to try on. Helene slumped before the mirror and complained: too tight, too narrow, too yucky. She wanted dresses with breast darts in them, even though she couldn't fill them.

"That's all right," said Belle. "The child has a right to her opinions. When we find the right dress, she'll shine like a star in it."

I stopped protesting and watched, wishing I'd had Belle to mother me. The Mama I remembered refused to sew the rose petal costume for my second grade play. Instead, Papa came to school and, squished into one of those tiny desks with his knees past his elbows and straight pins clamped between his lips, he'd folded and sewed my red crepe paper costume. But this wasn't Mama; this was Belle. Helene stood straight for her, finally picking a handsome blue velvet A-line that resembled the one Mama had bought for herself. Helene even tried on seven pairs of shoes, then Mama bought her a purse to match.

"That's for you to keep your money in when you become a famous actress."

ACTING LESSONS

At the register I whispered, "You're spending too much money, Belle. You're not getting paid for your performance."

Mama's eyes snapped with a fiery light. "You know, once upon a time I thought nobody loved me. I didn't have a mother or anyone to tell me I was special, except Sister Mary George, my English teacher. Oh, my classmates teased me something fierce when I snagged the lead in our senior play, 'The Blossoming of Mary Ann'."

She raised an eyebrow to see if Helene was paying attention. "See, this boy in my class acted so mean I absolutely hated him, only in the play I had to pretend we were in love. Well, Belle was good at pretending. She'd pretended all her life that things people said about her didn't matter. She pretended she was not the daughter of the most notorious moonshiner in the county. Every day she walked home from school pretending her mother was still alive and waiting for her."

Helene had stopped fidgeting and hung on Mama's every word, as did I, as did the customers who had maneuvered themselves to the clothes racks closest to the cash register.

"See, there's this part where they're arguing, and he tries to kiss her, then she slaps him. This boy complained to Sister Mary George, 'Kiss HER? I don't even like her!' I was so mad I thought either I'd kill him or die, but I just bided my time, waiting. Pretty soon that scene came around and I never even let him pucker up before I hauled off and slapped him. Oh, I slapped him good. I thought of every mean thing he'd ever said, and I slapped him so hard he fell and knocked the goldfish out of the bowl!"

Belle's bosom shook with laughter. Everyone laughed with her, including the clerk who'd stopped boxing the clothes. Helene leaned on the counter, smiling. Belle blushed at all the attention, then seized the opportunity for promotion. "Now at the ripe old age of seventy, I'll be appearing this Thursday in Sweet Bird of Youth, written by Tennessee Williams and directed by Mr. Sherman Bass in the big upstairs room at the Old Library. Curtain at 7:30. My name's Belle Fitzgerald. I'll be seventy years old on Thursday, and this is my debut."

The woman tallying Mama's purchases glanced at the name on the credit card. Mama gave a slow theatrical wink. She reached into her purse for her roll of tape. "Do you mind if I put a poster in the window?"

The clerk posted the notice for her. Mama scooted her purchases off the counter, distributing piles to me and Helene as if we'd become Belle's assistants. We steered ourselves out the door and down the icy sidewalk, packages teetering in our arms. Helene had gotten the larger stack and the box with her new shoes slipped, falling onto the sidewalk. Mama waltzed by, saying casually, "Don't worry, honey. Some nice man will come along and pick that up for you."

Helene watched her grandmother, then glanced up and down the deserted streets. Blood rushed to my face as I set down my packages, picked up Helene's, and sandwiched it under her chin. When I sidled up to Mama, I hissed, "Don't tell her that. You know it's not true. The last thing I'd teach Helene is some unrealistic 'pink-lady' expectation."

Belle sniffed. "I never had to pick up a package in my life. And I met some awfully interesting men."

"That's never been my experience," I said.

I shifted the load of boxes under my chin to reach in my pocket for the car keys. I was thinking about my ex-husband Ray, about the different ways women manage to carry things. In the back seat, Helene had entered the mood of pretend. She leaned close to Mama, knotted her fist, and pressed it toward her grandmother, as if Mama were the grand dame and Helene the interviewer. I chauffeured with my eyes on the rear view mirror.

"Grandmother Belle, how old were you when you were in the play?"

"I was seventeen."

"Did you always want to be an actress?"

"All my life." Belle adjusted her scarf, as if a cadre of photographers would arrive any minute. "My stage was a tree stump in the back yard. My mother's chickens were my first audience."

"And did people like your first play?"

"Well," Mama said, "I never found out. The week we were to open, the war broke out. We'd been hearing things on the radio, waiting for something to happen. When it did, every man in town enlisted, including the leading man. So my friend Betty and I moved to California to work in the sheet metal factory. And that was that."

"You mean you were never in the play?"

"So much for having some man pick up your packages," I muttered.

"It wasn't a total loss," Mama said. "I got to slap Buddy Hopper."

"Buddy Hopper? The one you're in this play with?"

Mama's back seat laugh sounded wicked. "After all these years, he doesn't remember me. He thinks I'm Belle Fitzgerald."

By Tuesday afternoon, it had started to feel like a party. Under the pretense of buying lottery tickets, Papa and I made a run to the liquor store. Sherman Bass came out the 'In' door carrying a six-pack of Stroh's. While Papa shopped, I lingered outside and talked to Sherman, who was strapping his beer onto an old milk crate tied to his bicycle.

"Your mother's a trip," he said, shaking his head.

"Yeah, she's all in a tizzy, plastering posters all over town. Papa's calling the relatives. Opening night ought to be a full house."

"Belle's exuberant," he agreed. "She's about to drive us crazy giving the actors lessons back stage. I got kinda rough with her the other night during tech rehearsal. She kept whispering the other actors' lines whenever they paused to breathe."

I flushed, feeling embarrassed. "Oh God, I'm sorry ..."

He shrugged. "Oh, she'll be fine. Don't worry."

Wednesday afternoon Mama, Helene, and I drove to the New You Beauty Parlor so Mama could have her hair done by my friend Chloe, who'd been cast as the ingénue. A single mother raising two daughters alone, Chloe worked nearly sixty hours a week and had little time to rehearse. I held the book for them while they ran lines.

Chloe combed and snipped nonchalantly through each word as Mama fiercely eyed her plastic caped self in the mirror, wet head full of metal clips and neck wrapped in tight gauze. "What you want to go back to is your clean, unashamed youth. And you can't." Her eyes flashed in the mirror, and she laughed. "Well, that's the truth now. Isn't it, Heavenly?"

Chloe lifted the cigarette in the ashtray that she and Mama were sharing. "I kinda like being the girl a fellah comes back to, for a change," Chloe said, "even if it is only for two weekends."

"Oh, it's exciting!" Mama squealed, observing Chloe and herself in the salon mirror as if they were already on stage and Helene and I in our waiting room chairs were part of the audience. "I can't believe I'm doing what I always dreamed. Did you know I'll be seventy years old tomorrow?"

"My lord, woman!" exclaimed Chloe. She flopped the bangs into Mama's eyes, re-parted, and clipped. "You couldn't possibly be seventy. You look fabulous. I hope I look as good as you when I'm seventy."

Mama smiled. "Oh, but you should have seen me in my heyday." She glanced at Helene, who only pretended to flip through the dog-earred issue of *Young Miss*. "I was the girl Otto Preminger wanted to put on his Christmas parade float."

Chloe stopped combing. "Get outta here! Really?"

"Who's Otto Preminger?" Helene asked.

Mama's eyes found Helene in the mirror. "He was a big movie producer. Had all the famous movie stars in his stable. I met him at this party once and he came over to me, saying, 'Your face! Your face!'"

"Go on! I can't believe it!" Chloe glanced at me and gave a wink. The other customers turned in their chairs until the beauticians turned their chins back, whispering, "Hold still!"

"Let's just say he wasn't looking at my face! He tried to get me to ride on his parade float as the Christmas angel, wearing nothing but this shiny piece of gauze. Can you imagine?" She addressed me in the mirror. "Imagine your mother riding through the streets of Hollywood like Lady Godiva dressed in practically nothing but a smile!"

"Well, what did you say?" Chloe asked. She pulled down the black electric clippers to shave the back of Mama's neck.

"What do you think? I told him, 'no.'"

"I swear, Mrs. Davis, you could have been a star ..."

Mama smiled nostalgically as Chloe flipped the button on the clippers. The salon burst into noisy silence. When Mama finished, Helene hopped into the chair. Chloe raked the tangles with her fingers, scolding, "Child, don't you ever comb your hair?" Helene didn't answer. She was busy waving her hands, making wide eyes, smiles, shrugs, and grimaces in the mirror like she'd seen Mama do.

"Are you and that handsome leading man still seeing each other?" Mama asked Chloe.

Chloe sighed. "Not exactly. Hank and I broke up." Mama looked surprised, but Chloe shrugged. "You know how it goes ... Guys are the worst prima donnas. He's being a big baby about it."

While Mama dressed for her last rehearsal, Papa and I hid downstairs, wrapping presents. Helene decorated a banner that read: "Happy Birthday and Welcome Back." In a jumble of dusty boxes in the storage room, Papa found a color-tinted photo that took my breath away. Inside the mahogany and gold-tipped frame resided the eighteen-year-old girl, draped in crushed velvet, who'd once been asked to ride on Otto Preminger's float. "This goes on the mantle," Papa said.

The morning of opening night Sherman Bass called. Belle answered in her breathy, Southern voice, but her voice soon fell to a hushed monotone. "Oh ... Oh ... Oh my ..."

Papa and I paused over our grapefruits straining to hear.

"What happened?" She breathed into the phone, punctuating her silence with 'Mm-hmm's.' "I don't know what to say. I'm so sorry.... "

"Somebody died," Papa speculated.

"Let me know if I can do anything," Mama said.

"Just sick," I whispered to Papa.

"Okay. Well, thanks for calling."

Back in the kitchen, Mama picked up her empty plate and Papa's. She laid the dishes in the sink and returned with more coffee; she collected the egg-stained forks and slid them into the gray dishwater, then she sat down with a cigarette and tried to smoke it. After a few puffs, she realized it wasn't lit. She searched the table for matches she didn't find.

"I'll get a light," I said, jumping to my feet. The suspense was killing me.

"So who died?" Papa asked.

Mama looked at him funny. "Nobody. Why do you think somebody died? It's only the play was cancelled."

"Oh," Papa said, and looked sad as if somebody had died.

"What happened?" I asked, sitting back down and forgetting Mama's light. I pulled a Carlton from her pack and held it smokeless in my hand. Mama got up and rummaged through the hutch for some matches, then lit her cigarette and mine.

"The leading man quit."

"Chloe's boyfriend?"

"Quit!" Papa shouted.

Mama nodded.

"Well, I'll be. That's the second time that's happened to you!"

"Well, it wasn't the same man." Mama puffed her cigarette and swept the breakfast crumbs into her hands. "I guess the theatre and I were never meant to be."

"That's a shame." Papa's voice sounded froggy on Mama's behalf.

She sipped her coffee and glanced out the window. A light snow was falling, the first of the season. "Oh, it was just a little bitty old part. It's not like I was born to play Aunt Nonnie or anything. I'm going to miss being Belle, though." The coffee cup clattered onto the saucer as if it had fallen of its own accord from the sky. The noise surprised me. "I was living on wild dreams, on nothing but wild dreams," she recited. "Oh what the hell ..." she spat. "I'm seventy years old. I'm lucky I could remember my own name, much less my lines."

Papa and I told the relatives what had happened. Everyone agreed to come to the house instead of the theatre. After all, it was still Mama's birthday. We took her to her favorite restaurant by the river, which advertised itself as "The Best Seafood Restaurant By a Dam Site." Mostly I sat, staring outside as the weak sun glittered across an endless parade of ice-covered driftwood. The logs floated lazily, then picked up speed, going faster until, caught in the current, they hurled over the dam.

Once home, Papa and I hurried through the house, arranging tables and flowers, laying out food, carrying in folding chairs and an ice chest full of champagne. As the guests arrived, Mama swept out of the bedroom to answer the door. Instead of wearing her new dress, she appeared in the flowered K-Mart shift, clunky white shoes, and tattered parasol that were the costume of Aunt Nonnie.

"Mama, why on earth?" I asked.

"Honey," she said. "I wouldn't want to disappoint my fans."

That night Mama recited all thirty-six lines from her canceled performance. Her family applauded adoringly. After her third vodka tonic, she stopped in the living room to declare, "I am so happy ... God bless you!"

When the final guest departed, Papa and Mama sat dazed, two sets of puffy ankles propped up on folding chairs amid crushed paper napkins and guttered out candles. I bustled around the living room, dumping abandoned plates of food into a garbage bag. Helene sprawled in front of the television. Pointing to the actress beside David Letterman, she declared, "One of these days, that'll be me sitting up there. Right, Grandmama?"

Mama said nothing.

"Isn't that right, Belle?" I asked.

I turned to face Mama in her lazy boy, but she wasn't paying the television or us any attention. She looked tired and unexpectedly seventy as she sipped her drink and gazed off into the darkened snowy street. In a while, Papa, slumped over and asleep, began to snore, then Mama picked herself up real quiet, lifted the portrait from the mantle, and slid it into the credenza drawer.

GOING WEST

Papa is thinking about going west; in fact, he is obsessed with it. Ever since he watched that National Geographic program on the hidden life of the desert, all he talks about are the saguaro with their long arms uplifted and the old man cacti growing long white beards. He isn't actually going anywhere. It takes an unusually long time for him just to get off the couch and go down the hall to the bathroom. He shuffles along the carpet in thick-soled black shoes, gathering a monumental static charge. I can tell when he's reached the bathroom okay because he shouts, "Shit! Goddamn shit!" when he touches the metal doorknob.

We all have our obsessions. Papa's is going west. Mine is electricity. I'm sitting in the kitchen with a voice-activated tape recorder that won't work because somebody left it on and ran down the batteries. In front of me lies a shoebox full of batteries that Papa has saved. They were down in the basement with all the other junk hoarded over a lifetime of seventy-odd years: yellowed newspapers, rusted paper clips, inkless ballpoint pens. There are hundreds of inaudible cassette recordings full of board meeting minutes dating back to a time when he was director of the Kentucky Children's Institute and knew where he was going.

I remember coming home from the hospital with Mama after Papa's first really terrible stroke, although he'd been having little ones off and on for years. She stood washing dishes while I, her graying, middle-aged daughter, sat on the kitchen step stool, crying.

"He's not ever coming back, is he?" I asked.

"Oh, he's coming back, all right." She sounded angry about it. She was scouring fried meat from the bottom of a Teflon pan, using a wire brush.

"Well, his body might be coining back. But he's not coming back. Not the man who was my father."

"It's hard to say," Mama answered. "My husband ... Your father ... I don't even know if we're talking about the same man." She looked down at the Teflon pan, its scoured, scratched bottom now revealing shiny metal. She lifted it out of the water and threw it in the garbage.

"I always knew he'd die and leave me with all that shit in the basement to clean out," she said. "I've told him for years to just throw all that old junk away. What does he need it for? Old office memos and Rolodexes and files for an Institute that fell apart fifteen years ago." She rinsed the food traces out of the metal sink, dumped in some Comet, and started scrubbing.

"When he crumpled down on his knees in church on Sunday and couldn't get up, well, I thought that's a good way to die. You couldn't ask for a better death than down on your knees in the house of the Lord."

"But, he didn't die, Mama."

She dried her hands and flung the dishtowel over the stove handle. "None of this," she said, "is what I thought it would be."

I hear the toilet flush down the hall, but it'll take Papa another twenty minutes to get himself together and back to his spot on the living room sofa, the side covered with forest green towels. Mama laid them down because he often spills his drink, or fouls himself.

One by one I drop the batteries into the empty chamber, alternating positive and negative poles. The machine still doesn't work. It could be one out of four, or four out of four dead batteries, or a broken machine, or me putting the batteries in wrong. I go through the whole process again changing the pattern, checking myself, then testing the batteries. Each one has to be tested in a different combination with all the others. There are forty-seven double-A batteries in this shoebox. For all I know they're all dead. For all I know it's the machine that is broken. I won't be able to tell until I get to the end of this process. I tried going out to buy four new batteries, but that's when Papa disappeared into the basement for a long time, then came up with his shoe box.

"Waste not, want not," he said.

In the living room I can hear the television blabbering in the corner like an idiot child. There's a stack of shiny metal pie plates glinting on the counter and another stack of plastic tubs so washed and faded it's impossible to tell what the original containers were for. Even from in here I can smell the dust that's collected on all the silk and straw flowers Mama has placed all over the house to make things look genteel and hospitable. I feel like shrieking and throwing everything away. It's all garbage, garbage, garbage, garbage....

I'm so tired, sorting batteries, sitting under this humming fluorescent light above the kitchen table. I've never been this tired in my life. In the middle of the night I wake up in Mama's basement room in a panic, thinking, I'm *wasting my life*! And I can't go back to sleep. I sit in the dark for hours, staring into closets full of clothes like other selves I haven't worn in twenty years, or holding onto year-old letters from my ex-husband in envelopes I haven't ever opened, or staring at my daughter while she sleeps beside me, still surprised eight years after her sudden appearance in my life.

No, Mama. It's not what I thought it would be either.

Mama's gone now and isn't coming back for a while. She's taking a little vacation. She's recharging her batteries. I actually said that the other day. Some telephone solicitor called asking for "the lady of the house." I said, "She's not here. She's recharging her batteries." I shouldn't joke about such things. It's hard to believe a person would actually pay someone to run bolts of electricity through her brain, just so she could stop thinking the same old thoughts, just so she could learn to forget.

For Papa down on his knees, forgetting was easy. God hit him with a bolt of lightning. But now it's only certain things he can't remember, like zipping his fly, or turning off the stove, or how to put on a pair of pants. He still remembers Uncle George Washington blowing taps on a battered bugle at sunset in 1924 in Papa's boyhood hometown of Eminence. "Uncle George Bush was seventy-two years old, the town's oldest living Negro Union soldier," Papa told me last night. He'd been watching the evening news on television, mixing campaign headlines with personal history. I don't bother to correct him anymore.

Mama, on the other hand, never forgets anything, and that's been the source of her trouble all along. What she remembers has gotten so far under her skin, she's paying a hospital to make her forget. One day she went to see Father Billy at the church and when her appointment ended, she refused to leave. She kept sitting on the sofa, staring at an ornamental Jesus on his coffee table, mumbling. "I'm as depressed as Pearl S. Buck." Mama made me read *The Good Earth* once, but now I've forgotten what it was about. It's amazing how much you can forget without even trying.

I don't think I'm ever going to get this tape recorder to work. And I really wanted to record Mama and Papa's stories to find out what happened when they were young. I want to know. I wasn't there half the time, so that part I'm not expected to know. Some of the time, I was too little to remember. The rest is just fact and image compressed into a tight little wad of memory, a fist that refuses to unfurl. I'm supposed to remember these family stories, so I can pass them on to my daughter. I don't know why I'm saying that. When has my daughter ever listened to a thing I've said?

I sound like Mama. She's been saying that for years. Some things you don't need to tape record; they just scratch themselves into your brain against your will until one day you find yourself saying them. I do sound like Mama, exactly like Mama; so much so that when I answer her phone even her sisters think it's Mama. I wonder if history repeats itself because it's encoded in the DNA. Will I get old and forget like Papa, or forget like Mama? I don't sleep any more. I'm tired. I've never been so tired in my life. I throw up my hands in frustration. Why am I sitting at this table hour after hour fooling with this tape recorder and a bunch of dead batteries? If only three of forty-seven batteries were good, I still couldn't get the damn thing to work. I'm wasting my time — wasting it.

Papa has situated himself back on the sofa. I go in to sit down beside him. He thumbs through a mail order catalog of Native American art, jewelry, paintings, and posters.

"I've always wanted to go to the desert," he says. "Abby Rippey lives on an Indian reservation, you know. She used to work for me. She moved out there when she retired. I got a letter from her at Christmas." Now he's getting choked up, weeping. It happens whenever he remembers anything, anything at all. Papa never used to cry. He saved up his tears for his old age. Mama used hers while she was young.

"We ought to go see her some time," Papa says, wiping his nose.

"That'd be fun," I say, "except we'd have to go through Texas."

He chuckles a bit. 'Going through Texas' is what we call any long, boring spell in life. One day after things fell apart and I'd come back home, I referred to my marriage as going through Texas. Papa laughed then, too. Of course, neither of us has ever been to Texas, although my ex-husband once lived there. Papa calls him 'Lard-Ass,' even though he's the skinniest man alive. Papa says, "Did Lard-Ass send the child support check?" My Papa loves me.

"I love you, Papa," I say, and throw my arms around his neck just like I did as a child, even though my hair is nearly as gray as his is. He stops wiping his nose, and looks at me. The way he looks at me seems like he doesn't remember quite who I am.

"I don't want you to think I'm stupid," he says. "I don't want you telling people I'm stupid."

I think I said it at the grocery store one day — said it to someone in a moment of frustration and because my heart was breaking. Some neighbor stopped me between the aisles of tampons and Metamucil to ask how my father was. I said, "He's old and stupid. And I can't bear it." Now it feels like Papa has slapped me. I can't take back what I said. That's how I feel. I can't make it right, but I can soften the blow. I can say it in a way that doesn't hurt to remember. I look him in the eye and say, "My Papa was never stupid."

A few days ago when I saw Mama at the hospital without her eye makeup, she looked positively blank and lidless as a fish gazing at me. She didn't remember me. She called my daughter by my name. The nurse said that kind of memory loss was a temporary thing. She was sitting up in bed, wearing a blue cotton-tie gown and a serenity prayer necklace one of us kids had given her a couple of years ago after Papa had his stroke. It says:

> Lord, grant me the serenity to accept
> what I *can not* change,
> the courage to change the things I *can*,
> *and* the wisdom to know the difference.

I was glad to see Mama, even though she didn't entirely see me. In a way it was good. I could be a totally different daughter for her. For a while the past was gone — that meant my past too. She'd forgotten our fights, our bitterness, the way I ran off one day and just left her, how I didn't come back for nearly fifteen years. I *thought* that maybe I could start all over, saying the things I wanted her to remember, the things that really were true. "It's me. I'm your daughter, Mama. And I love you. I have always loved you."

She looked at me and said, "Well, maybe that's true. I don't really know you, but you say you're my daughter, so I guess I believe you. But I do know one thing." She smiled and the weariness disappeared from her face. "God loves me. I'm certain of that."

"I'm glad you're certain, Mama."

She pursed her lips. "Well, maybe I'm not entirely certain," she said. "But it just makes things a lot easier to take if I believe it."

I was pretty sure then I wasn't the child who had given her the necklace, but I wished I had been. I wish I could remember. So much of my life I've failed to remember, whole chunks of it disappearing between the lunch boxes and the appointments and everything else. I'm terrified of the idea that those who don't remember history are doomed to repeat it. Of course, some things I'd prefer to never have happened. Some things I'd really like to forget. And some day I will. I'll either forget them like Papa, or I'll forget them like Mama.

One day last week while I was folding laundry, my daughter came and stood by me. She gave me that accusatory look while I was leaning over the dryer, sorting out whose underwear was whose — her grandfather's, her grandmother's, hers, mine. I do a lot of sorting these days. We've been 'visiting' her grandparents for about two years now. I know she wants to go home. I want to go home, too, if I can ever remember where it is. My daughter stood accusing me, her arms crossed over her chest, sunken, joyless.

"This is boring," she said.

She doesn't know the joke about going through Texas. In the silence that followed, we had a conversation though neither of us said anything. The conversation went like this:

"Did you ever love my father?"
"I'm sure I did. But at this point, I think I've forgotten."
"Then did you hate him?"
"I guess I did. But I've forgotten that, too."

When I was nine I asked Mama these same questions, sitting on the edge of her bed while she smoked a cigarette with the chenille bedspread pulled up to her neck. My father sat in the living room pretending to read. Not knowing what to say, I kept looking.

"What are you looking at?" Mama demanded and pulled the covers over her head.

Thirty years later, standing beside me in my mother's laundry room, my daughter was staring, demanding an answer. Her belly pooched over the waistband of her pants — the clothes we'd arrived in already outgrown. What has happened to the time? She kept her eyes leveled on me; I kept folding laundry.

"Boring," she said.

"Look," I said, throwing a pair of shredded undies into the trash.

"Sometimes we don't always get the things we want. Most of the time we don't. There's not a whole lot we can do about it. Your grandfather didn't ask to have a stroke, and your grandmother didn't ask ... well, for any of it. But we're running out of time here. My parents are old. You do understand that, don't you?"

She walked out of the room, but she probably understood it better than I thought because when I tucked her into bed that night, she asked, "Do you really think people are born over and over again? You know, like do they come back to life somewhere after they die?" She'd been watching "Unsolved Mysteries" on television again. I could tell.

"You mean reincarnation?"

I thought about Papa and how it always seemed as if I'd known him forever, as if I'd always loved him, and how it seemed at every turn I was just scratching the surface of what could be known about Mama. Not that I loved him more than her, but that I sympathized with him a little better. Maybe I really am too much like her.

"I suppose I do," I answered.

Then my daughter turned away from me and broke my heart. She said, "I don't ever want to be born again. I couldn't stand it. It's so awful. It's boring." And I realized my shame. I'd never made it any better for my child. With every decision I'd made for my own reasons, or because I thought it was the right thing to do, for her I'd only made things worse. She knew all about going through Texas.

Late in the night when I wake up the light is on in the kitchen. The coffee pot sits empty on the counter. Freshly brewed coffee streams onto the kitchen floor. Papa sits in his spot in the living room hunched over a travel atlas, peering through a dirty magnifying glass. I thrust the pot under the coffee maker and there in my nightgown in the middle of the night, I mop the kitchen floor. I don't say anything. I don't have to; my face says it all. Papa comes in and sees me. It takes a few minutes for him to register what I'm doing and why I'm doing it. He starts to say something, but he coughs instead, his eyes tearing. I know he knows and I don't want him to say anything.

I mop furiously. Mama will be coming home next week, or most of Mama. The rest of her they say will eventually come back some time later. I don't want her coming home to a stained sticky floor.

He calls my name softly. I interrupt.

"There's still some coffee," I say. "I'll bring you some in a minute. Just sit down." I regret the last sentence. It sounds like a parent scolding a child.

When I bring him the coffee, he lays his head on my shoulder. We're like some old couple with insomnia sitting on the sofa in the middle of the night, worrying about wasting electricity. I guess it's better than staring into the dark.

"Are you tired?" I ask.

"Yes. I'm tired. I'm so tired. I could just about die. I'm tired of being old and useless and stupid. I can't remember anything and I hurt all over. I'm so tired, I can't stand it any more."

Now I'm the one who is crying.

"I know," I whisper. "And I'm so sorry."

He sits up. He drinks his coffee. He lets me rub the age spots on his hands. Finally, he coughs and shows me the map where he has highlighted the highways going west through Kansas and Colorado, then dipping south into New Mexico, carefully skirting Texas. He tells me he wants to see the sunset in colors — rose, peach and purple against the mesas. I tell him I want to see the fulgurites, those sandy cauterized glass bones of desert lightning.

He looks at me a long moment, then says, "Actually, I've always wanted to see the blue bells of East Texas."

I smile. "I suppose we have to go through Texas sometime. We might as well see the blue bells."

He uncaps a different highlighter and begins marking an alternate route. I think about driving west with Papa, and Mama, and my daughter. I try not to think about having to buy new tires or how many pit stops traveling with a child and two old people would mean. I try to think about the way the land would smell after a rain. That would be some time next spring — if Mama's come back in one piece and Papa's still here, if he hasn't made his trip west already.

One of these days he will. After that I'll help Mama sort out all the things in the basement: old office files and newspapers, forgotten record albums, mismatched dishes — all the inevitable waste produced by simply living. Who knows what she'll want to keep by then? I'll haul it all out, just like Mama wants me to do. Then I'll pack it all into my basement, just like Papa did. That will be then. For now, I'm thinking about packing the car with blankets and boxed chicken lunches, going west, through Texas with Papa.

THE GOLD IN HIS MOUTH

In Marshall's Restaurant hometown lawyers banter with judges. Tradesmen jab thumbs at each other and lean over their luncheon specials. For five and a quarter you get fried catfish, kale greens, mashed potatoes, pickled beets and fried corn bread. The food always comes garnished with the talk of a sassy waitress.

Papa and I sit in a window booth, squeezing ourselves in between the cracked, red Naugahyde and beet-stained Formica table. I give him the seat that offers a view onto the street; in case he feels like waving to anyone he recognizes walking by. Papa hasn't been out of the house in months. Mama refuses to take him. She won't even let him open the mail anymore because he keeps ordering Publisher's Clearinghouse Sweepstakes magazines, trying to win a million dollars. When she buys gas for the car, he takes money out of her purse and buys lottery tickets.

The last time we took him to the big Wal-Mart on the other side of town, she rushed him over to a tiny luncheonette table, saying, "You just sit there until I come back. And don't you drink any coffee. You'll just have to go pee-pee, and you'll never make it. It's all the way over on the other side of the building. You'll wet yourself and make a mess. Don't you leave or go wandering off either, and make me come find you. I'm not hunting the store after you again."

Mama never looked at him while she spoke. She was looking around to see how her performance was being received by me, by the Wal-Mart employees and customers. I'm ashamed to say I walked over to the sale blouses and pretended I didn't know her.

Most everyone else had sense enough to keep their eyes averted and hurry by, except for the clerk peeping around from behind the display of rotating, shriveled hot dogs. Papa never said anything, but his eyes glazed over. It only made him look retarded, trying to pretend that he didn't know who she was.

"Don't let him have any coffee," Mama warned the girl behind the counter. "He'll just have to pee-pee again, and he can't hold it." She grabbed her crotch in a gesture that seemed more obscene than explanatory. "He'll make a mess for you to clean up. And spill his coffee, too, you know. He's just like a child. He can't remember a thing I've told him the million-teenth time. Every time he comes out of the bathroom I have to say, 'Zip it up. Zip your pants. Zip 'em up!' and he won't do it. He makes me so durn mad, I could kill him."

Mama gritted her teeth and shook both fists in the air. Plastic bags full of merchandise she was returning hung from her wrists and banged the glass case full of chili, cheese, and leathery hot dog buns. "It's Alzheimer's," she shouted at the clerk. "He's a real mess, I tell you what."

Glaring at Papa, she shook her wrinkled finger. "No coffee."

After she left, the Wal-Mart clerk became absorbed in wiping the counter with a wet, gray rag, afraid to look at the old man who'd somehow been left in her charge. He stared straight ahead and said softly to no one in particular, "It was a stroke. I've had three strokes."

At Marshall's Restaurant we sit in a sunny window by the front door. The first thing we order is coffee. I'm not ashamed to be out with Papa, even when he forgets. I want him to know I'm not ashamed. I'm just not saying much because every word feels different, more jagged, suspended inside my mouth. Yesterday I broke a tooth. I touch my tongue to the new crevice there, mapping its edges.

We've just gotten him a shave and hair cut at Cliff's Barber Shop where everything smells of soap lather, old men and peppermint. After four decades Cliff still only charges Papa a dollar for a haircut and shave. I watch him perform this rite of depilation with the tenderness of a long friendship, though Papa stares straight ahead and neither man says a word. Now, smelling sweet, with his collar buttoned up to his chin and his hands folded on the Formica table, Papa looks almost dapper. If only Nat King Cole, instead of Clint Black, were playing on the radio, I'd ask Papa to get up and dance with me.

Papa's past dancing, anyway. His knees are shot, but it's his eyes that worry me. They seem full of strange yearning light, yet somehow empty like a house abandoned in the night. Maybe it's age; maybe it's despair. He sits hunched over the table on his elbows as if reading words that I can't see. I turn my menu between us so he can read it. The waitresses type new menus each morning. They're not very good spellers.

"Oh look!" Papa says finally, "*stewt* tomatoes. Wonder what they know that we don't."

The women at Marshall's cook like my grandmother. Nostalgia is why we eat here. On summer Sundays when my cousins came from Ohio, my brothers and I picked over half a peck of fat, hairy blackberries growing along the fence rows behind Grandmama's house. I stood with her by the stove, making cobbler, adding sugar and stirring the dark, bubbling fruit. In the corner on a stool sat Granddaddy, sullen, vacant-eyed and speechless after his sixth stroke. The only intelligible words he said were, "Shit, goddamn it, shit," whenever his cigarette burned down to the filter and scalded his fingers. Grandmama cooked and laughed at her own bawdy jokes. I ate fried, battered squash that she had shaped for me into kitties and butterflies. The corn bread batter she spiced with oodles of pepper. Her flour-feathered hands turned out four trays of angel biscuits. On the stove bubbled stewed tomatoes with green peppers, onions and sugar. White corn sliced from the ear with a knife and fried, lay in the iron skillet like rows of sawed-off teeth. After I was grown and had moved away from Kentucky, that was the home I missed — a home already gone, its tribe dispersed, weeds grown up between the yellow roses and peonies.

When the waitress comes, Papa and I order, substituting stewed tomatoes for beets, and adding peach cobbler for dessert. We sip our coffees. Papa's is heavily whitened with nondairy creamer and saccharin, as if he'd forgotten his mother's coffee. I touch my tongue to the gap in my mouth, remembering the way my tooth crumbled, how it seemed a small, hard truth wedged between my gum and tongue. It was a revelation of loss, as if overnight I'd turned into the old woman I'd been waiting to become.

Papa hunches over the table and blows his coffee. He reaches into his pocket and starts rummaging his hand around, making feeble scratching noises. It looks as if he's playing with himself. In the back of my mind I hear Mama's warning: "He doesn't know how to behave. You can't take him anywhere." The flailing and scratching grows louder. Now it's as if he's wrestling a ground squirrel trapped in his pocket that he can't figure out how to get out. I pretend absorption in something inside my purse. Finally, Papa works his hand free and suddenly bangs his tight fist onto the table.

"Looka here," he says, but the fist is still closed. He stares at his hand, observing each finger one at a time, trying to make them unfurl. It's like watching a time-lapsed film of a crocus blooming. Inside his palm lies a molten lump of metal. "That came out of my mouth!" He laughs childlike, his tongue wagging, spittle collecting at the corners of his lips.

"It's gold!" he shouts gleefully, as if I didn't know.

"Well, I declare."

"What do you think it's worth?"

"A hundred dollars," I guess.

"No. Maybe four hundred or more ... and it came right out of my mouth." His voice slides from gleeful shout to throaty whisper.

THE GOLD IN HIS MOUTH

He laughs, then cries. A tear plunks into his coffee. He can't help it; it's what he does these days when he feels emotion, when he's feeling anything at all.

"So you think it'll cover lunch?" I ask.

"Yeah," he says, still weepy, working his hand back toward his pocket. He fishes in the other pants pocket and comes up with a wadded handkerchief and a quarter. "I used to have another quarter to go with that," he says, "but I lost it. Your mother always said money had a way of slipping through my fingers."

I smile. Since his strokes he's lost feeling in his left hand and in his feet. I reach across the table to hold Papa's hand, which can not hold mine in return. I spy the gold from his teeth lying half-hidden under his palm beside the wadded up handkerchief. I point to it as the food comes.

"You'd better put that back in your pocket," I say.

"Yeah," he agrees, cupping his hand around it. "I don't want to forget to stop at the jeweler's and ask Mr. Roberts how much this is worth."

"So what're you going to do with your four hundred dollars?" I ask.

"I'm going to get my Ph.D.," he says.

"Shit," I say, reaching for napkins as the coffee Papa just spilled slides over the table onto my leg. Sometimes Papa's hands are wild birds that fly away from him before he can catch them. I dab and dab, grab more napkins. The spilled coffee's a blessing. I don't have to say a thing.

"I'm sorry," he says.

"Don't worry. It's just coffee." The waitress hustles over with a rag and helps out, refills his cup. I stuff moist napkins into the table corner.

"Do you want me to cut up your fish?"

I cut up his fish, careful to remove the bones. Papa bows his head to say grace, his eyes squinting hard, trying to remember, rambling on. He mixes up the words for the blessing of the meal with the burial for the dead. Same difference I think. I say "Amen," when it sounds like he's finished.

We eat as if we are hungry. All of a sudden I feel on display, sitting in a brightly lit window seat with an old man who can't keep his left hand out of his mashed potatoes. It's not that I'm ashamed. I simply couldn't bear to have someone who used to know him the way he was walk down the street and see him. I don't want them laughing at or feeling sorry for my father.

I eat with my head tilted, so the hot food avoids my tooth. My tongue is sore and ragged, bleeding from trying to pronounce words around this jagged filling. This tooth reminds me to keep my mouth shut. I'm learning to make accommodations: a lisped word, a tilted head, a less explosive fricative, a gesture to replace a sentence, a kindness to replace frustration.

When I went to the house this morning Mama was taking one of her vinegar baths, and Papa was nowhere to be found. The screen door was open, the television blaring. I got back into the car and started driving.

I don't really blame Papa for trying to escape. Ours was never a comfortable house. Mama kept the drapes closed all day, saying she was allergic to sunlight, but I knew it was because there were dead things inside our house that she didn't want the neighbors to see. For the better part of middle school I played ghost, hiding in closets, under the sofa, climbing into empty cabinets downstairs, lying curled up in a fetal position breathing in the piney dark. I'd hear Papa come in and lift the top of the broken cabinet-style phonograph, take out the vodka and pour himself a drink, then shut the lid quietly before he disappeared into the furnace room. Everybody at our house was well practiced at being dead.

To me Papa's jailbreak seems understandable. I did it myself once, twenty years ago when there was nothing left in town to miss, except Papa. I'd driven west in search of The Rest of My Life. What began in youthful expectation ended in mid-life divorce. I'd always been afraid Papa would die while I was gone, but I came home, and Papa's still here. And so am I for now. I'm waiting for Papa to die.

This afternoon I found Papa out on the six-lane highway trying to cross the street, headed for the Interstate. Cars changing lanes around him honked and swerved. I pulled up beside him, leaned over, and opened the passenger side door.

"Where're you off to?" I asked.

I knew he didn't recognize me. He watched me with his mouth open, his body intent on breathing, his fingers fluttering. He coughed, closing his pale glazed-over eyes, listening to trucks whining down the highway. He squinted, rolling his eyes backward and tilting his face a bit, as if in the back of his head there was a blackboard with his destination written there.

"Papa, get in. I'll take you where you need to go."

He shuffled his feet, looking up and down the road, searching for some less-traveled road hidden behind the summer haze. Then his face melted into a kind of resolve I thought I understood, where accepting a ride with a stranger going anywhere was better than staying where you'd been. Papa tried to climb into my car face forward on his hands and knees, the way as a child I used to crawl through the darkened storm sewer tunnels, headed toward the light. I flicked on the hazard flashers and got out of the car. Taking his thin shoulders I backed him out gently, stood him up, and turned him around to face me. His gaze wandered across my face, and then he gave me a droopy smile.

"Papa, let me help you. You have to turn around and back into the car seat. Lift up your head and look at me. Now go slow. I want you to start to sit down." He hesitated. "It's okay. The seat is right behind you. You just have to lean forward a little and sit."

I put my hand on his head to keep him from banging it on the car frame. His fuzzy gray hair felt like a dandelion puff. "Watch your head now."

"That's where I'm going," he said. "To get my hair cut." He lowered himself into the car and sat. I sighed, relieved. Cars kept honking and swerving. I heard someone cursing.

"Fine. I'll take you," I said. "Now lift up your feet."

Papa lifted his feet one at a time as if marching. "Papa, lift them up and put them on the floor of the car." He grasped one leg at a time and lifted, gathering his legs like firewood. "Okay. Now move your hand. Don't hang onto the car roof. I've got to close this door. I don't want to catch your hand in the door. Papa, put your hand in your lap. That's it."

I buckled the seat belt and closed the door.

When we got to the house I found Mama running between the bathroom and bedroom, toweling off, creaming her skin, grunting busily with her jaw set. She was wearing a bra and a crotchless panty girdle that she'd gouged with scissors so as not to struggle with her girdle every time she went to the bathroom. Mama always did have her own ideas about things.

"Mama, I'm taking Papa out for a while. We'll be back."

"Remind him to get his hair cut," she said.

"He knows."

She hadn't noticed Papa's escape, and I wasn't going to tell her. That last time we went shopping at Wal-Mart, Papa got tired of waiting for us and decided to explore the store. We searched for him for over an hour, calling his name over the P.A. system. Mama finally found him staring into the mirrors in the bathroom home improvement section. She screamed at him, throwing her packages onto the floor. "Goddamn it! I can't take you anywhere. You refuse to do a thing I ask you. If you're going to act like a two-year-old, then I'm going to treat you like one. I'm going right this minute to buy you a leash and harness."

That time Papa stared right back. "Why don't you buy a bit while you're at it?" he asked. 'You can put it in my mouth and jerk it whenever you want to watch me bleed."

Mama raised her hand to slap him and I stepped between, trying to make myself look large when I'd rather have fallen through a crack in the floor. "Stop it!" I shouted. "Just stop. Both

THE GOLD IN HIS MOUTH

of you. We're in Wal-Mart, for God's sake. Let's just get the hell out of here and go home."

I realize I've been staring out the restaurant window as if it were a giant TV screen. I don't know where my mind goes these days. It drifts in and out like Papa's. I've been sitting with my hand clapped over my mouth, like one of those See-no-Hear-no-Speak-no-Evil monkeys.

"What's the matter?" Papa asks.

"Aw nothing. I just broke a tooth."

"Your tooth!" Papa blinks several times, then reaches into his pockets again, fishing in the right pocket, fumbling around in the left. He stuffs his hand down his pants waistband. He's fishing in there, too.

"Papa, what're you doing?"

"I'm looking for my gold. I thought I put it in my pocket."

"It's right here." I point to where he has left it on the table between us, half-hidden under the mound of wet, shredded and wadded up napkins. He slides the lump of metal across the table toward me.

"Here," he says.

"What's that for?"

"Your tooth. I'm giving it to you."

"I thought you were going to get your Ph.D. with it!"

"Why, hell!" Papa shouts. "This won't buy a Ph.D. I'm giving it to you. It's about four hundred dollars, maybe more ... It came right out of my mouth."

"You know, this is like a bad joke. Stealing the gold out of your father's mouth."

"You're not stealing it. I'm giving it to you."

"You might need it for something."

"I need to give it to you."

Our hands push the metal back and forth across the table. I notice the lawyers at the next table have stopped talking and eating; they watch us instead. I hate a damn lawyer, so I say in a loud voice, "We're negotiating my inheritance. Now just go on and eat your lunch, okay?"

They laugh. I turn back to Papa.

"Hang on to it, Papa. We'll go see Mr. Roberts in a minute. Anyway, you're all the gold I could ever want."

My Papa used to tell stories, endless stories rolling easily off his tongue. Sitting with his sisters around Grandmama's dining room table, he'd laugh and bang his hands, making glasses of ice tinkle and silverware rattle. Ears of corn quivered in their bowls of butter. My childhood's joy was constructed from Papa's memories.

I'd lie on my back on the floor beneath Grandmama's cherry table, looking up into a tabletop wooden sky, listening to the textured sounds of history, of people, small towns and times I never knew. Words shuttled back and forth like strings weaving a web of story. Sunlight pierced the windows casting squares of patchwork illumination onto the pine wood floor. The stories Papa and his sisters wove came to resemble the tattered cloth spread over the table, drooping over its edge and collecting into lacy pools of white light in their laps.

Papa did not so much gossip as he told mythologies, tales of divine suffering enacted by men and women. I'd never heard of Demeter and Persephone, but I'd heard the story of Mr. Moody. Weeks after the telling, my mind wandered back to this widowed law clerk from Eminence, Papa's boyhood town. Mr. Moody walked five miles every day rain or shine to his wife's grave. He walked and plucked the roadside flowers — ironweed, crown vetch and daisies, raggedy robins, wild bee balm, yarrow and larkspur. He keened and walked, weaving floral wreaths. Five miles every day, many thousand flowers a year, five decades of sorrow ... I imagined the ocean of tears he'd shed, all the shoes worn out in grief, and how he teetered between green memorial lawns and the abyss of each fresh grave when it appeared. In my mind's eye I watched him sob and mourn each passing, whether he knew the deceased or not, tears like dirt clods falling over each coffin.

The lives of these characters transformed into golden threads for the tapestry of Papa's recall. I heard these stories again and again. Each time Papa pulled the thread back through, the cloth of story became stronger.

Across the table from him, my Aunt Libby extended the tale by saying. "You know, Charles Robert, you forgot the best part. Remember Miss Minnie, who played the organ at the movie house on Saturday?"

"Good God, yes!" cried Papa. "Miss Minnie was absolutely in love with Mr. Moody. She worshipped the ground he walked on. I can see her now in my father's store, buying the lace for the wedding dress she was making, awaiting the time Mr. Moody quit grieving, finally noticed her and asked her to marry him. Of course, he paid her no attention…"

On and on Papa told his stories of heroism, lost loves and sacrifice while squares of daylight slid from white to gold, crept from the floor onto the far wall, and then were gone. I'd fall asleep beneath the table at my Papa's feet. I dreamed I wore an amazing coat made from the pages of a book — an ankle-length coat, long-sleeved and buttonless, a coat made entirely of language inside and out.

I ask Papa, "What was the story about Miss Minnie?"

"Miss Minnie?"

"You know, the one who was in love with Mr. Moody."

"What about her?"

"Didn't she play the piano at the movie house?"

"I don't remember," he says, looking out the window at nothing on the street. The lawyers have paid their tabs and gone. The waitresses bus the last tables. It's late. Papa's tired. I know better than to push, but I push. It's like I'm on a mission to recover what's been lost.

"She played the piano at the movie house on Saturdays …"

Papa trembles a little and coughs. He sits looking at me. I look back. I'm waiting, waiting ...

"My mother used to play the organ at church on Sunday," he says. "She played the organ for the white church and the black church, too." Now his eyes scan the fly-speckled ceiling and the whirring black fans in his ritual of remembering. "I can see her standing in her nightgown in the dining room. She was a beautiful woman then, with her long black hair let down and the violin tucked under her chin. She used to sing ... She used to sing ..."

He stops. His voice breaks off and his thin, white fingers flail at his face, trying to take off his glasses. The glasses cord tangles and twists around his nose. I grab another napkin off the table, untangle him, and take off his glasses so he can wipe his eyes.

"I don't remember," he sobs, dabbing his face. "I can't remember ... what my mother's voice sounded like ..."

I keep handing him napkins for his eyes, napkins for his nose. He cries while I rake my tongue over my jagged tooth as punishment. Finally, Papa says he's going to the bathroom. He balls up his fists on either side of his body. Using his arms as braces, he begins rocking and rocking, trying to get up, rocking furiously until at last he lurches forward and sways uncertainly. He topples at first, then catches himself and slowly rises to a stand. He shuffles down the linoleum to the restroom, watching his feet. Right, left, right, left. That his feet move at all seems a surprise.

He stays in the restroom long enough for me to finish another cup of coffee and sit clutching an empty cup. The waitresses wipe down the counter and tables, talking about where their husbands will go fishing tonight for tomorrow's catfish special. Our waitress picks up the wet napkins from the table, stuffs them in my cup and carries it off. I gather our things: the wadded handkerchief, car keys, purse, and Papa's eyeglasses.

I pay our tab as Papa comes out. He's embarrassed not to have any money and offers me his gold again. I shake my head, and we amble on down the street. Papa scuffs his shoes along the sidewalk, balancing on my arm. His touch is as feathery as a caterpillar crawling on my skin. I watch our passing reflections in the abandoned store fronts, our disconnected heads and torsos, arms and legs, moving between the boarded up window panes.

Mr. Roberts' jewelry store smells of cigars and Florida water. The stopped wall clocks and clip-on colored paste earrings belie the opulence of the severed, black velveteen hand modeling diamond rings in the window. From his pockets Papa pulls out his empty eyeglasses case, shredded tissues, half a roll of breath mints, and empty wallet, laying them on the glass countertop. "I've got this gold, here ... somewhere..." Papa begins. Mr. Roberts gives us his thin Time-is-Money smile.

"Wait here," I say.

I sprint across the street and down the sidewalk to the restaurant where the window shade is drawn and the door locked. I bang it. I bang it with my fist. I bang, bang, shouting "Hey! Let me in. Somebody let me in!" the way I once pleaded outside the door of my mother's house. It was dark. I was three and she locked me out for not sleeping in my bed. "Hey!" I shout, "I'm sorry. Please. Open the door. Somebody, please ..."

Pain surges up the side of my face. One of the waitresses, carpet sweeper in hand, peeps under the window shade and unlocks the door. "Gracious!" she says. I hurry past her to look under the table where Papa and I sat, around the broken seats, between the cushions, behind the booth, under the sugar dispensers, then inside the bathroom on the floor, behind the toilet, around the sink.

"What'd you lose?"

"The gold from my father's mouth."

The waitress shakes her head. "Well, I declare. I heard him try to give it to you twice today. You should have taken it then."

I smile and point to the tied plastic garbage bag. "Do you mind?"

She shakes her head no. I rummage through everybody's cigarette butts and lunch leavings, the half-nibbled beets, the fish and chicken bones, the congealed gravy around lumps of mashed potatoes. I stick my hand in some cobbler slime, and there, in a wad of paper napkins, I find it. It seems a most precious thing.

I hurry back to the jewelry store. The chime tinkles over my head, but Papa's not there. "Sorry," I tell Mr. Roberts. I run a block and turn left in time to see Papa shuffling down the street, headed for the bridge over the river — I sprint up alongside him, my knees crunching with every step, my teeth aching each time I inhale. "Hey!" I shout.

He turns.

"What're you doing?" I ask.

"I was going for the police," he says.

I open his hand and return my Papa's gold. "Here it is! See. I found it!" His knotty fingers can not grip and close around it. I take it and put it back in my pocket.

"Tell you what, I'll keep it until we get home."

We walk toward the car. I feel his labored breathing, and my mind turns toward home, hurrying to take him out of this heat. At the jewelry store, Papa stops. "I'll only be a minute," he says. "I just want to know what it's worth."

I sigh and take the gold from my pocket. "I'll wait," I say, opening the door for him, listening to its chime. Papa disappears inside. On the sidewalk I watch the traffic lights change their colors. No cars come by, but the lights blink caution anyway. The air feels weighted down in its humidity. I peer through the summer haze hanging near the river, a damp, fuzzy blanket of air that reeks of fish and fermented whisky from the distilleries downstream.

Papa comes out, and I ask, "Do you want me to hang on to that for you?"

"I don't have it," he says. "I sold it."

"You sold it? Well, how much did you get?"

"Thirty-seven dollars."

Inside my mouth I feel the enormous abyss into which every word I imagine uttering falls.

"You were right not to take it. It wasn't worth anything at all."

I lead him to the car. We are silent, our eyes focused inward to glimpse a diminishing past, as if life were a landscape seen out the window of a speeding car. I open the door and turn him to face me, to lead him down into the seat. He sees me. I know he sees me. "Before we go home," I ask, "is there anything you want?"

"Yeah," he says. "There's lots of things I want, but you can't get any of them for me."

As I walk around behind the car, I take a full breath through my teeth, a deep breath welcoming the sharp pain. It roars through my mouth, down my neck, and around inside my head. I don't even flinch.

So I do it again.

PAPA IN PENTIMENTO

STORM WARNING

The lights blinked off and on as if the universe had decided to send Papa a message, sort of the way truckers flash their lights to warn of a wreck ahead or a police car hidden behind cedars. The stabbing pain in his head, the flashing lights meant: *Pay attention! Look out, you fool!* Papa barreled down the same road as if the message weren't meant for him.

He mixed another drink, two, or three, ate whatever tasted good, as long as it was cooked with lots of sugar and butter. "Sure, I'm taking the medicine," he told the doctor. He meant *all* the medicine — whatever was in the cabinet. If he remembered it was there, he took it. Down in the basement with tins of sardines, Roquefort on crackers, and double martinis, he listened to scratchy Glen Miller records spin webs of song through the night.

He were getting on in years, forgetting things.

All through the last decade the signs appeared, but Papa never mentioned them, so we never noticed that he was having ministrokes. Once when he and Mama visited me in Colorado, I'd sent him to the nearest store for a gallon of milk before dinner. He didn't return for three hours; the store was six blocks away. When he finally returned, nonchalantly swinging a plastic sack with Roquefort, Ritz crackers, and a gallon of milk, Mama stopped him and sniffed his breath. In truth, he'd gotten lost.

On Sunday morning the danger signal flashed one last time. I wish I'd been there when the stroke happened to reach down and lift him back up. I tried to imagine that day that he suffered a stroke in church — how the earthquake in his brain reorganized the terrain of his mind. Papa moved through the dark, bumping into things as hazy and indistinct as memories. Nothing appeared where it should be. He seemed to be in a church, but he no longer heard the priest intoning or felt Mama kneeling beside him. The words of the prayer book began to blur, then the words caught fire and curled the pages, turning them to ash in his hands. The nave hummed and buzzed as the church plunged into frozen darkness. He swam beneath the surface in green, murky light; a book of prayer fell from his hands.

Down on his knees, he could not get up. He might have thought it was a dream and when he woke, everything would slide back from gray-green to full color. Then he would tell us how odd things seemed, as if he'd been taken to the dark side of the moon. But Papa did not wake. The church where he slumped fell silent. Men in white floated down the aisle, slowly, processionally — perhaps they were angels. On a litter they carried him away. I've heard God works in mysterious ways.

No matter how much he bargained with God, or tried to convince himself that he would change — or how hard he tried to persuade the doctors, or Mama, or me — it had already been decided. Papa never came home the same.

PAPA'S BRAIN

Papa lay in a hospital bed staring up, as if God's face appeared on the ceiling. Panting through his droopy mouth, his eyes scanning the air, he tried to locate the sound of voices he heard. In the hall the doctors and Mama stood inspecting his MRI. She'd never seen a brain scan before, and she found the whole idea fascinating.

"See that white in the mid-section of his brain? Between the two lobes?"

"There?" Mama pointed.

"Those are dead brain cells."

"That's *all* dead?" She gasped, terrified and fascinated. "Is that from the stroke?"

"No ma'am. They're old cells. They've been dead a long time."

"Alzheimer's?"

"Maybe," he said. "Did he ever suffer a brain injury?"

"A brain injury ..." Mama pursed her lips. "Maybe in the war?" she asked.

"Was your husband a heavy drinker?" She clamped her jaw tight and nodded. "Whatever the case," the doctor said, "drinking won't have helped the situation."

HIDING (1967)

I thought I knew all the hiding places: in the small kitchen cabinet above the stove, in the store room cabinets behind the pressure cooker, in his tomato juice, in the living room behind the painting of a violin surrounded by books, in the back of his bedroom closet, in the cabinet of a broken record player in the basement, in the tool shed behind the lawn mower, behind a sliding panel in the lower drawer of his mahogany desk at the office, in the trunk of his car in a brown leather photographer's case, in a metal tumbler of ice sweating on the counter.

"Don't touch that," Papa said. "That's my water...."

Mama kept the drapes closed all day long because she said she couldn't take the sunlight; I believed it was because there were dead things inside our house that she didn't want the neighbors to see. We were like those daytime soap opera vampires; we excelled at pretending to be dead. Papa gave up his dream of becoming an artist before any of us were born — and down in the basement one brother lay on his back immobile in the dark under the purple haze of a Jimi Hendrix experience, while upstairs the other brother sat on the edge of his bed, blowing the fox call he'd gotten for Christmas, making sounds like a wounded rabbit, imagining himself hunted, maimed, and dying, while big tears plopped off the ridges of his cheeks.

Alone for the better part of a day I played "Dark Shadows," crawling into storm sewers to write poems, or spying on my family from hiding places in closets and under furniture. From the top of a willow I spied on the neighborhood boys playing football.

Downstairs in the basement I curled up inside an empty cabinet, with my knees against my chin, just breathing in the dark. If I lay very still I could hear someone speaking: a neighbor calling her Pomeranian, Papa whispering the instructions of whatever he was building to himself, sometimes the voice belonged to Mama. In her upstairs bedroom above my head, Mama talked to her mother, a grandmother I knew only as a sepia-toned photograph of a tired-looking sixteen-year-old girl in braids pinned over the crown of her head. She died alone in a mental hospital when Mama was thirteen. She died still cowering from her drunken husband's abuse. In her own way Mama played "Dark Shadows," lying in her bedroom with the curtains closed.

When Mama's father drank he did terrible things. When my father drank he laughed and did goofy things, like pretending he was in a speakeasy while he listened to Duke Ellington jazz and Moms Mabley comedy albums. In the grocery store he re-enacted the Winn Dixie commercial by pretending to be an armored knight as he rode up and down the aisles on a shiny shopping cart. Singing the store jingle "Come save! Come save!" he chased me through the detergent aisle with a broomstick lance under his arm.

Lying in the wooden storage cabinets underneath the basement stairs, I'd hear him open the basement door and step heavily down the creaky wooden stairs. He lifted the top of the old broken cabinet-style record player, took out the vodka bottle, and poured a drink. Softly, quietly, he shut the lid before going into the utility room to hammer something together — another bookcase, another cabinet, a broken whatever. Mama's high heels clicked across the linoleum in the kitchen upstairs. Looking for me, or for one of my brothers, she walked in circles from room to room while my father hammered and hummed tuneless notes.

Tap, tap, tap went the hammer.

Rap, rap, rap went the shoes.

All together the noise made a tinny symphony like the sounds of tiny nails being driven into coffins.

HEAD OUT

I stood in the hall on one large, shiny, black linoleum square under a harsh florescent light. Mama and the doctor stood across from each other on large waxed white squares. For a moment I imagined all of us as a living game of checkers. I wasn't sure who had the next move. In my father's hospital room the sheets rattled as he tried to get out of bed. A month had passed. A suitcase lay open on one of the stiff, green Naugahyde chairs. My brother Danny was taking things out and laying things in: dress shoes out, house slippers in; blue cotton shirt out, night shirt in. My father got out of bed and wandered the room, opening closets, sticking his head out the door, going back in, turning on the television, turning it off, coming back out into the hall in his half-opened robe.

Mama and the doctor kept talking.

It was stroke. It was Alzheimer's. It was myocardial infarction. It was hardened arteries, diabetes, and something else. "So basically," she said, "he's still sick, but he's not sick enough to die, so you're sending him home for me to take care of." Whenever Mama felt frightened she raised her voice. It was her way of whistling in the dark. "I can't take care of him. I'm not a nurse. I don't know what I'm supposed to do."

Papa licked his lips, stuck his hands in his pockets, and pulled out an empty cellophane candy wrapper. He looked at it, curiously. "What do you need?" I asked.

"I wasn't looking for anything," he said. I began to wonder what he was looking for.

"We'll be done in a minute," I said.

He said nothing, but began to meander barefoot down the hall, the belt of his blue robe following him like a tail. "Where do you think you're going?"

"Home," he said.

"We are going home. Just wait a minute. We have to talk to the doctor first. And we have to finish packing up your things, then go down to the pharmacy to get your medication. After that we have to check you out, but before we do any of that, we have to get you dressed."

Papa gave me a blank look. "I've been ready," he said, then looked down at his bare feet and pulled the blue robe closed. He stood in the hall and picked at the Band-Aid on the back of his hand covering the bruise where his recent IV had been. "I think I'll go and find your mother," he said, then walked off in the opposite direction toward the elevator.

I turned him back toward his room.

Mama cocked her head, sighed audibly for the doctor, and jerked her thumb toward Papa. She looked like a hitchhiker stranded in a hospital corridor. "That's what you call ready to head home?!" She was not happy.

The doctor repeated his recommendations for a rehabilitation therapy schedule, noting how often Papa would need outpatient therapy, how long the sessions would continue, what the therapists would do there, how Mama should follow up at home, when to give Papa what medication, and what progress to expect. The words spun around each other: "Four times a day, three times a day, at bedtime, with food, with or without food, it doesn't matter, as needed. Coumadin, nitroglycerin, trimazerapan, colchicine, elavil, 80 mg. aspirin ..."

All Mama saw was a long, snowy drive over an hour each way to the rehab center, three times a week for she didn't know how many months or years. The rest of her life stretched out like a Siberian Highway. Any other woman might have burst into tears, but Mama stamped her foot, raised her voice, and shouted, "Stop. Stop. Stop!" She tried staring down the doctor with fiery looks. In a moment they were joined by a physical therapist with a clipboard, an intern, and another doctor.

My brother and I managed to get Papa out of his robe and into his street clothes. Then a nurse made him sit in the wheelchair; she strapped him in for good measure. When we were ready, Danny wheeled him down the hall. Mama followed behind them, taking slow, painful steps while plastic bags of medical files and her heavy black purse banged against her thighs. She sighed and stared straight ahead like a soldier headed to battle. Harsh florescent lights glittered across the silver hair on top of her head. She looked as if any moment she would burst into flame.

"I'll drive," Papa said, reaching for the keys.

"That's OK," my brother said. "I'll drive."

PAPA AT HOME

After two weeks in intensive care Papa came home and sat down on the sofa. The golden years to which he and Mama had looked forward now extended no further than the glow of a globe of light in the living room under which Papa sat every night. Slowly, chaotically, he read his letters from Ed McMahon declaring him the certain winner of a sweepstakes prize, if he licked this particular stamp, and put it on that particular card that he'd accidentally crumpled in his hand, and onto which he scrawled his name as he ordered trial subscriptions of magazines that would cost him no money for six months. He never remembered to cancel, telling the company why he was not satisfied.

With a damp palm, Papa smoothed flat the crumpled envelopes and cards, then squinted at the fine print that he struggled to read and understand, regardless of whether or not his glasses were perched on top of his head. To ease his frustration, he'd get up and fix some popcorn, scratching the copper bottom of the heavy pan over the top of the heated metal coils on the stove, sometimes accidentally catching the towel he was holding on fire, dumping the towel in the sink, then opening the window and throwing the smoke detector out on the back porch before it went off and woke up Mama. Then he'd finally relax to David Letterman or one of the late night shows, sitting under the globe of yellow lamplight and eating popcorn.

Mama hated it — especially the popcorn — because he was ruining her Revereware pots and her stove burners, filling the house with smoke, and besides he'd get popcorn all over the floor, or go to bed with the back door wide open. Whenever he woke up, she woke up. "I'm such a light sleeper!" she'd said. She'd hear him walking through the house and think: *He'll turn on the stove and forget it; he'll burn the house down, or leave the door unlocked.*

Papa hated it when she woke up because the only time he ever felt like himself was when she was asleep. It had become a kind of game with them — Papa, seeing how quiet he could be and how much he could do before she woke; and Mama, seeing if she could wake up and catch him doing something. Separately, each complained to me of being exhausted because neither of them was sleeping. Although they slept in separate rooms, they constantly listened for each other to make a wrong move. In the morning over breakfast, as I tried to get everyone fed and Helene dressed for school, each complained to me about the other. Because I battled my own demons of insomnia, I hardly slept either and had heard them all night long, both walking along the hall, floorboards creaking above my head.

One night Papa must have found himself in Mama's room, remembering what life was like when they first married. He might have remembered sleeping next to her and seeing her hand on the sheet, the wedding ring shining in the moonlight. So he lifted the sheet to lie beside her a moment so he could remember it again.

Her eyes flashed open.

"What are you doing?" she demanded.

"I'm going to bed," he said.

"Well, you're in the wrong room. Go back to your own bed."

She pulled the covers over herself and turned away.

Later I heard the sound of metal scratching against metal and knew Papa was upstairs making popcorn, making a mess that Mama would complain about in the morning if I didn't go up there and help him. While Helene slept I tiptoed upstairs to sit on the sofa, watch TV and eat popcorn in the middle of the night.

DOWN THERE ALONE

That spring Papa developed the habit of sneaking into the basement for hours at a time, as if he were hiding in the corners of his own mind. Again and again, night after night, he rummaged through old boxes, combed through his personal effects and slowly gathered his things: stacks of video cassette tapes, maps of trips out west, wads of rolled up rubber bands, gummed file folder labels stuck to each other, psychiatric social work textbooks and a copy of Margaret Mead's *Growing Up in Samoa* that he'd practically read to disintegration.

"I think your father reads dirty magazines down there," Mama confided to me. "He thinks I won't know."

Papa blew the dust off Frank Sinatra, Eddie Arnold, and Danny Kaye record albums that he placed on the hi-fi to play, except he couldn't figure out how the turntable worked, or if it worked anymore, or whether it was even plugged in. He left the records taken out of their sleeves sitting on top of each other on top of his desk, then turned to a collection of color slides from trips Francine Bates, a church member, had taken through Turkey, Egypt, Greece and Morocco in 1955. He kept her slides among his things, but he couldn't remember why. Papa was in Australia during the "Late Great Unpleasantness," as he called it, only he couldn't find any pictures of that. He used to have one picture of himself on the beach outside Sydney with an army buddy — a man whose name he no longer remembered — holding seashells to their nipples like nacreous, fat, spiral breasts.

Papa hoarded things: whittled wooden chains, cancelled postage stamps, coins, tape-recorded board meetings, glass jelly jars, postcards from places he'd never been and newspaper clippings about disasters. He forgot what they were supposed to remind him of.

"I lock the door to keep him from going down there," Mama complained in May. "He could fall and die and I'd never hear him. I'd have to wait for the smell to know anything at all had happened to him."

In the back of the closet beside the furnace in the utility room, Papa discovered old framed photographs of mountain children he thought he'd lost, canvases that he'd painted forty years ago during his tenure in the college art club, along with his pastels and paper, his pencil sketches, his tubes of oil paint. On the cold, concrete floor beside the boxes of Christmas ornaments and wrapping paper that he'd pulled out of the way, Papa paged through the linoleum cut proofs of Christmas cards he'd made when he was in college to send to family and friends back home. He had never sent them because he had printed the image on the wrong side of all fifty folded cards.

"He's going to die and leave me with all that junk in the basement to clean up," Mama complained in June, tugging at her hair, and then shaking empty fists in the air. "Ay, ya, ay!"

Papa fingered paint-stiffened camel hair brushes and dropped crumbling charcoal pieces into a box that he carried upstairs. For months he'd been gathering charcoal and pastels, bringing them up one by one to hide under his bed. He got up in the middle of the night to work on his charcoal drawing. Mama wanted to know what the hell he had managed to smear all over his night clothes, some black stuff that wouldn't come clean no matter how many times she washed his pajamas.

One July afternoon Papa proudly showed me his latest art project: a pastel picture of his future tombstone. Behind the red granite stone, a mauve, crimson, and ochre sunset bloomed as deep purple clouds gathered on the horizon.

"So, what do you think?" he asked me.

THINGS TURNED UPSIDE DOWN (1974)

Papa's secretary Bonita studied Edgar Cayce and practiced astrology. Whenever Mercury went retrograde, she double-checked her appointment books, her typing and Papa's correspondence. She kept her pulse on not only the office schedules, but its money, personnel files, the typing pool dramatics and the interoffice shenanigans; she also cast Papa's horoscope and gave Mama a copy.

One afternoon during the after-hours vodka and tonic in Papa's office, Bonita characterized Papa as a taciturn, tight-lipped triple Scorpio. "For example, she said, "he never tells us anything at work — not about the lost funding, or about the upset workers, or about the striking miners in the mountains, or about his taking another salary cut. I find it out the hard way, by filing his correspondence or listening to the board minutes on tape."

She and Mama sat side by side like graying sisters on the green sofa in Papa's office nearest the liquor that he kept stored in an old wooden ice box, and to which Bonita had a key. Home from college and working in Papa's office that summer, I sat in his leather high-backed swivel chair underneath an abstract canvas that I'd painted that fall in art class and abandoned. Papa had found it downstairs, carried it to the framers, then hung it behind his desk where it glowed in its own special light like a sort of ghostly yellow, orange and ochre halo above Papa's head. I hadn't had the nerve to tell him he'd hung it upside down.

On this particular day, Papa busily emptied the office trash, a task he never considered menial, since that was his way to find out what work his employees had done for the day.

Mama agreed with Bonita. "That's about right at home, too," she said. "He never tells us anything. He just pretends it isn't happening. He goes out in the yard in the middle of the night and hammers rocks, or cuts marble into tiny tiles with a drill saw. In the middle of the night, he'll be out there drinking martinis alone, shouldering the burden alone. I guess he expects me to shoulder mine, too. 'I don't want to hear your complaints and paranoia,' he tells me. 'I've got troubles of my own.' He never tells me anything."

Our family loved Bonita. She was a hard woman to fool, even though Papa sometimes tried. Finally, she got tired of his increasing temper tantrums and quit. By that time Papa was drinking Bloody Marys for breakfast, fighting with Mama and wrecking a few cars. I had already moved to Colorado, though my brother Alan at that time lived in the basement, and he remembered their fights. When he told me about it, I hadn't believed him. I hadn't believed it until I came home, found the suitcases on the bed, and saw the bruises on Mama's neck. I thought she would leave him then. She'd packed as if she were going to leave; but she never did. I can't remember if I thought she was acting brave, noble, or just plain stupid. That was the first time I'd ever seen Papa cry.

Shortly after the incident Papa retired from the office. He tried turning over the wheel of his ship to a younger captain, but the new director he'd chosen was an outsider. Within months of Papa's announced retirement half of the staff in the Appalachian counties had quit their jobs. One by one the office staff in the home office left, and finally the board members closed and locked the doors. Papa returned for a brief while, pretending like nothing had happened. Slowly he moved things from his office into our basement: boxes of paper clips, double A batteries, and typewriter ribbons. A ring of keys in his desk downstairs opened file boxes that he'd first warehoused, then abandoned, then were dumped by the warehouse owner and no longer existed.

When Papa began to slip, misremember, mistake, or misconstrue, we couldn't tell if he was letting the cat out of the bag, inventing a new life for himself, or just misinformed about his old one. He woke from an afternoon nap, put on his navy suit and a tie before heading into the kitchen. "I've got to call the social welfare office before it closes," Papa announced. "There's a woman sleeping with her three children under the Singing Bridge by the old post office. I've got to call Jeanette, I mean Lola Smith, no, I mean Martin Lacy. No, that other man, what's his name? It isn't right that people should live under bridges."

"What woman under the bridge?" I asked him.

"What are you talking about?" Mama demanded.

"Damn it," Papa shouted. "Haven't you been listening to a word I said?"

We believed that he believed there was a woman under the bridge whose children were cold and wet, but we were no help at all. I came to see that time and again. No one could help Papa with dates or names, or events, or streets, or signs, or facts, or feelings, or the past, or anything, since none of us knew what he thought about things, or where he'd been, or what he'd done, or who he really was, for that matter. Who my father was seemed locked inside one of his warehouses in a rusty metal filing cabinet, but even he could not tell us anymore which key opened the cabinet or the warehouse door.

THE ROAD HOME

On the first of May I drove Papa through Henry County. He had a voice-activated tape recorder bulging in his shirt pocket. It whirred along with the spinning sound of tires, the whistle of wind through the open car windows, and the erratic bird calls from the alfalfa fields we passed. Papa talked in sentences that wound around and around themselves like country roads, sometimes coming out where he started, veering off into unexpected alleys, or ending up in an entirely different direction. I let him talk. That week on my list of things to do:

1. Pack and move to my own apartment
2. Get Papa out of the house …

He wanted to drive. I wouldn't let him. He insisted he knew where we were going. In a way he did; we were going back in time, going home, to New Castle, to the crossroads of Papa's memory. You got there by driving some distance on a narrow road between generations of walnut trees and limestone fences built without mortar. We traveled the humid late spring day without urgency. Going nowhere we found we had arrived at the courthouse square in a half-forgotten town of houses with a few wide gray porches and white columns with blistered paint.

I looked for a place to park the car. Papa kept talking.

"And the people in the town resembled their names. There were the Landers who owned a lot of land, and Mr. Moody who was … Oh my God, he cried all the time, walking up and down the road to the cemetery, gathering flowers and weaving them into wreaths for his wife's grave. Twenty years! And then on that corner was an old lady I used to carry coal for in the winter — named Mrs. Nutall and … Oh my God, I swear, was she ever a nut …"

I helped Papa out of the car; he was still talking with his head down, reciting names into his shirt pocket. I could barely hear him. On a bench under a sparsely leafed-out maple tree we drank Cokes with shaved ice in paper cups. Dogs on a mission padded solo down the sidewalk, looking right then left, their metal tags jingling on their collars under their chins. Young mothers in tennis shoes pushed baby strollers over uneven sidewalks as they jogged around the town square. The tape recorder whirred on in Papa's pocket.

"That was the second house we lived in and we lived there the longest. Father called it Poverty Row, but we called it home. It was really Property Row and I remember I'd walk to school, cutting under the fence across that field down there … Or I'd play hooky with one of my friends and we'd go down to the branch at Drennon Springs, get into mud up to our knees. Oh my God. There was an old man who lived down there and used to catch fish barehanded...."

Papa told one story, then another, then another, then another. Each story bled into the next. He gossiped about his classmates, his family, his neighbors. He licked his lips savoring the memory of cat-head biscuits or barn door bread "dripping with butter clear down your elbows." He was animated, recalling every detail of people's lives, of half-remembered, half-invented conversations.

"... He set that shotgun down between his knees, and Boom! Blew his face half off, his chin and his nose. Good Lord! What a mess. We picked teeth out of that ceiling for a week ..."

I pulled out a notebook and added to my list of things to do:

3. Buy cleaning supplies.
4. Transcribe Papa's stories.

HIS SHOE POLISH (1961)

Saturday night. Perry Como crooned beneath a spotlight on TV. Or maybe it was Carole Burnett and Tim Conway. I remember sitting in front of an old black and white TV, trying to stay up past my bedtime.

"Can I polish your shoes for church, Daddy?"

Papa brought me his box full of rattling shoe polish tins. The hinged lid opened to reveal several half-full tins of Kiwi polish — brown and black and white and brown and more brown. The reddish brown stained bristles of the brush inside felt soft and smelled heavy, oily and sweet — a smell not altogether unpleasant, a smell I came to identify almost entirely with my love for my father.

I slipped old ragged once-white cotton socks over my hands — a trick I learned after so many years of Mama complaining come Sunday morning that she doesn't like seeing my hands and fingernails stained brown at the communion rail. I dipped the rag into one of the tins and began to dab and wipe.

Papa hurried to apply a layer of newspapers to the carpet in front of me. Mama doesn't like brown stains on her green carpet either. I sat for hours and polished shoes. Other people's shoes appeared: Mama's, my brothers', my own — a couple of pairs from each one, in fact. I polished, I polished and I polished.

Papa poured himself martinis mixed from the vodka he had stashed in the back of an old radio that stopped playing over a year ago. I stroked those brown shoes like they were a cat. I brushed long deep swipes. The bristles shushed until the motion and the shush-shushing made me tired, and I stopped.

Papa nudged me upstairs and I went straight to sleep.

MORNING COFFEE

I blinked. Three years streamed by, along with another small stroke, a bleeding ulcer, and the erasure of memories. I'd gotten into the habit of stopping by my parents' house on the way to work for a morning cup of coffee. I'd watch Papa shuffle around the kitchen in his bathrobe. He wore this janitor-sized ring of keys on a black coil that was somehow simultaneously stuffed inside his pocket, clipped to his wrist, and linked to his billfold, even though he'd just gotten out of bed. His hair reared up into a peak like a graying Lyle Lovett.

All glazed over from his medication and sleep, my father made coffee, and set it on the table steaming away in a cup ready for me. He must have poured it the minute he heard my car pull into the driveway. I like Papa's coffee much better than that powdered, granulated shit with plastic coffee creamer and artificial sweetener that I got from whatever school cafeteria where I was teaching. Papa made real coffee, despite the fact that he couldn't hit the water in the reservoir of the Mr. Coffee machine, so there was always a puddle of water on the floor that he busily mopped up as I walked in the door. Spilled coffee grounds floated around on top of the puddle. Since Papa can't tell right from left, up from down, or in from out anymore, the coffee filter clung precariously to its slot, and the pot sat cock-eyed on the hot plate, filled with soggy grounds.

When he went to the bathroom to dress, I nudged the coffee filter basket back in and mopped up the brown puddle with a paper towel before settling down to drink Papa's coffee.

MEMORIAL DAY

When I arrived to take Papa to the reunion, he was already shuffling down the sidewalk in bright summer sunlight, wearing a rain coat and sports cap. My arms were full of spyrea, japonica and pink and white peonies shedding petals that I'd picked from the yard. The sausage casserole Mama had made drooped in Papa's limp hands. "Don't drop that," I warned. "That's our admission ticket."

We left the summer-lit world behind us as we entered the darkness of the meeting hall, a pine-paneled room in a windowless community center. Under buzzing florescent lights were two tables filled with white-haired women and Papa — and now me — the annual gathering of Stocktons, Whites and Davises. On Memorial Day, pointing at fading photographs, we repeated the names of our ancestors: Della Maud Davis, Pearl America White, Richard Stockton, John J. Stockton, William Perry Davis… Most of whom now lay under the shaded grass in cemeteries in Alton, Eminence, and along Pea Ridge. It was these graves that the remaining fourteen clan members would visit that afternoon.

I walked around the room looking over shoulders of stout women in navy swiss dot dresses. My father forgot to introduce me. He forgot to introduce himself, but he was easily remembered. "Well, there's Maud's boy!" Papa sat on the cold metal folding chair and waited for something to happen. Cardboard boxes opened, old women coughed, and cracked, bent pictures lifted out of boxes. Stories grew legs and ran around the room. The women seemed to weave a silver net of words over top of Papa's head. I didn't know any of these people, so I put serving spoons in casserole dishes and scooped ice into plastic cups. After the photo parade, we got back into our cars and took a long drive into the country with our flowers.

My father used to tell me endless stories, now I can barely understand what he says. I walked with him across the uneven ground, dodging pillow stones, broken markers, clutching his elbow. He whispered. I leaned in close. At his grandmother's grave I set down the Mason jar full of pink and white peonies. He stood a moment, chin dropped toward the grass. Papa recited weak, breathy prayers in words he half-remembered, again mixing the rites of communion with the burial of the dead.

I said "Amen." It's all the same really. It's how we feel that matters.

ART CAMP

I had taken Papa to the senior citizens' center one morning and came again that afternoon to pick him up. Most of the people had gone for the day, leaving after lunch. Only a few regulars and Papa remained. I followed a fat woman in pink and starch as she bustled down the hall, hollering through the open doors as she went. "Mr. Davis, your daughter's come to take you home."

We found him sitting in the music room. With his two-liter Pepsi bottle bird feeder sitting on the table in front of him, Papa grinned, happy that his liver-spotted hands could do something, even though they no longer recalled how to tie shoes or how to push a shirt button through the cloth.

"What did you do all day?" I asked.

He worked over his memory with eyes closed, tongue darting to mouth corners, head askew on neck, limp gray forelock flopping. His eyes clamped tight, as if straining to repeat words writ large. He opened his eyes. "This and that," he said, gesturing toward the bird feeder.

A woman at the upright piano began to play hymns. Papa leaned back in his sofa. With hands peacefully pressed across his shirt front, he listened to the piano breathing some deep wind of memory. Perhaps he recalled his mother's hands fluttering over the ivories as she played for the Methodist church in his boyhood town of Eminence.

Papa opened his eyes, then closed them again, lost in deep listening. I felt the same rush of loneliness and irritation that I used to feel whenever I had to retrieve my daughter from day care and she refused to leave because she was having such a good time. I knew I'd put the bird feeder in my car, and then forget to remind Papa to take it in the house. The last time he came back from the senior citizens' center with a Popsicle stick birdhouse Mama exclaimed, "What's this mess? Like a kindergartener makes!" Then she threw it in the trash.

Waiting for Papa, I sat on the sofa beside him and closed my eyes. We listened to the music while I held his hand that refused his will to hold mine. Ahead of us the hallway was a long tunnel opening out to summer's empty white.

PECULIAR MORNINGS

The sky turned green like it does during tornado weather; last year's dead leaves whirled themselves into towers in the driveway between houses. When Mama showed up, I thought to myself, *maybe this, too, will blow over.*

While I washed dishes, she sat in the corner of my kitchen, sighing and picking at her skin. Over the last few months, she'd begun clawing herself to pieces — the skin on her fingers cracked, oozed, and bled. Trapped in her own skin, she was trying to claw her way out. The woman who once cowered in the basement during thunder storms, showed up at my house with Papa, and sat in the corner of my kitchen, sighing audibly. Her explosive, violent prayers sounded as if she were swearing, "Oh my dear Jesus, GOD! What a beautiful day!"

Papa leaned against the breakfast island and sloshed beer out of a coffee cup onto the floor. He says he had seen a woman on Oprah Winfrey who had died and gone to heaven twice. "Everyone on earth has a guardian angel," he said, impressed with her certainty. "She knew it for a fact."

Then Papa reminded me that he had been born dead, and his grandfather's mother revived him by holding him by his feet over a half-frozen rain barrel, then dunking him up and down in the icy water a few times. She tied a tablecloth around her waist and fastened it to hooks on to either side of the fireplace. For three days she sat with the baby on her lap inside a homemade incubator.

"Is that right?" I said, although he'd already told me the story.

"She was Cherokee, you know," Papa said. "And all she ever drank was boiled water."

"Jesus, God Almighty," Mama groaned. "It's gorgeous outside!" She rubbed her hands and clawed her neck. Her fingernails click-clicked on the table.

"She said there are demons in the world, too," Papa affirmed. "Your Aunt Violet used to see them running up and down Cherokee Park in Louisville." Beer, amber as pee, dribbled out of Papa's glass. I stooped to wipe it up.

That evening Mama, Papa and I attended a play, *The Kentucky Cycle,* at Bradford Theatre. I thought a theatre outing would be something the whole family could enjoy. Besides my friend Doug was such a fine actor that I wanted Mama and Papa to see him. He played a cycle of characters, from a noble coal miner to the villainous role of a man who captured an Indian woman, raped her and kept her from running away by cutting her hamstrings. His performance must have been convincing because when the play ended and the actors lined up for their obligatory grip-and-grin with the audience, Mama walked over to Doug and slapped his face hard in front of everyone, loudly exclaiming, "That's for my daughter!"

While Mama went for the car, Papa and I walked slowly out of the theatre. He tottered on the sidewalk, head down, telling me one of his secret desires for fifty years was ... During World War II in the institution in Australia, he was.... Papa moved so slowly and spoke so softly even though I bent my head to catch his words, I could barely hear him above the sound of Mama honking the car horn and telling us to hurry. All I could feel was Papa's breath in my ear.

"You know," he said, "During the war I wrote two plays."

In the car he spoke again about the things he wished he had done with his art. The puppets he had made during the war with the soldiers in an Australian military hospital. "Poor old fellows," he muttered. "The chaplain sent me to buy them art supplies, then we put on a puppet play I had written." He coughed and stared straight ahead, talking to no one. "I wish I'd done more with it."

From the back seat, I kept leaning forward, trying to hear his voice, which is so soft and adrift I can barely hear it over the sound of the tires rolling down the highway.

"Honey, sit back," Mama said. "I can't see out the rear view mirror."

THE PRETTIEST ROSE (1960)

I didn't tell Mama about the Mother's Day play the school was having because the teacher said it was supposed to be a surprise. It never occurred to me that if she had to make my costume, she should have been told about it. My Mama differed from other mothers in the neighborhood. My Mama didn't stay home with us and bake cookies, or watch television in her housecoat. My Mama dressed up and put on red lipstick because she had an important job as a secretary for the Press Secretary to the Governor. When I sprung the news on Mama the night before the play that I needed a rose petal costume and here was a list from the teacher of what to buy and instructions for sewing it, Mama hit the ceiling.

She did drive to Woolworth's Five and Dime for the red crepe paper and crinoline to go under the costume, but since it was the night before the play and twenty-five other roses had already been constructed by my classmates' mothers, we were out of luck.

Mama called my teacher at home and said, "My daughter will not be in the school play tomorrow. I work all day and I don't have time to make a costume. I can't even find any red crepe paper in town."

"But it's for Mother's Day!" Mrs. Harned exclaimed.

Mama was unimpressed. "If a play is supposed to be for my benefit, I shouldn't have to miss work and lose my pay just to make the costume."

Mrs. Harned insisted that I had to be in the play. "Mrs. Davis, she's the only child who knows all the lines and can sing all the words to the songs."

In the morning Papa, dressed in his business suit because he had an afternoon meeting, accompanied me to school. Crammed into a little wooden grade school desk with his knees up to his chin and straight pins sticking out of his mouth, Papa sewed the rose petal costume for my second grade play, using scraps from the other children's costume and working under the teacher's instructions.

That night I had the prettiest costume in the play.

THE WINDOW

Before her children could protest, Mama called the nursing home for a consultation. The intake nurse asked Papa how many children he had. After Papa said "four," instead of three, it wasn't long before he had moved into the old soldiers' home in Wilmore. He had been there a week by the time I came to see him. When I arrived, the suitcase of labeled shirts, underwear, books and socks that had accompanied him still wasn't completely unpacked. Papa sat on his bed staring at the tiny blank television that hung from the wall on a mechanical arm.

"Well, isn't this nice?" I said more cheerily than I intended.

"It's an old folks' home," he said.

I folded my coat over a pink vinyl chair — the kind easily wiped clean. "So how'd you sleep last night, Papa?"

He shook his head. "Not too good. I wish you could have heard those old fellows all night long on their walkers, racing up and down the hall."

I looked out the window at trees that only the day before had leafed out. Their fuzzy yellow-green crowns resembled pointillism, or perhaps it seemed so because I wasn't wearing my glasses. The red doors of a black tobacco barn on a hilltop sagged open as if someone had just left.

"What a great view," I mused. "Have you ever thought about painting it?"

Papa breathed through his nose in irritation.

"I passed an art room on the way in. Some guys down there were painting. It looked kind of fun."

"I gave that up," Papa said.

"I'm glad your father gave up painting," Mama said when I told her about the visit. "He was never very good. Maybe some people liked it, but he painted such unattractive things. Even his flowers were brooding and unhappy."

Later that summer I went to the art supply store and whispered the names of the oil paints in their white tubes: vermillion red, cadmium yellow, raw sienna, cobalt blue. Art is good therapy, I told myself. I picked up a camel hair brush and tickled its bristles across my cheek, remembering the odor of turpentine and linseed oil, the soft-lipped sound of colors kissing canvas and blending into sky.

PAPA IN PENTIMENTO

IN THE CLOSET

On the eve of my 25th high school reunion I sat on the upturned five-gallon bucket that Papa used to cook country hams in. Pawing through the closet for my yearbook, I parted the waterfall of out-of-fashion striped ties. Out came the empty tins that once held home-delivered potato chips on Wednesdays; on Saturdays, it held popcorn that Papa shook, rattled and rolled over the electric burners on Mama's stove. In the winter those same metal cans held fruitcakes Papa made for Christmas wrapped in whisky-soaked cheesecloth with a whisky-soaked pared apple slipped down in the center of the cake.

The color slides of Mrs. Bates's excursions circa 1940 were stored in metal boxes labeled Egypt, Greece, Rome, Turkey, and so on circling the globe. After buying her slides at an estate sale, Papa tucked her memories down in our basement, hoarding them as if they had been his own, or maybe he couldn't tell the difference. In the back of the closet stood picture frames, mat boards and paintings on canvas rolls, photographs, water colors, oil paintings, pastels, and linoleum block prints. The art Mama had called useless Papa abandoned like a dream that filled the back of his closet.

In a box with baby food jars of nails, picture hangers, and matting tacks, I found a few photographs of Papa. In one he looked like a G-man with cocked black felt hat, right hand slung in his pocket. In another he stood grinning in a ribbed cotton undershirt, the boxing gloves on his fists held too low to protect his face; his opponent, knees bent, seemed about to beat the crap out of him. In a third photo he stood with his arm around his mother, who wore a straw hat with a black ribbon. With pants rolled up to his knees, Papa had been splashing in a Romanesque fountain at Western Kentucky teacher's college, hair in a pompadour like a dark ocean wave on top of his head, with a half-curl that broke across his forehead, then fell down in his eyes, wet, black and shiny.

In the back of the closet facing the wall I discovered an impasto portrait of my mother. Holding her head in one hand, a cigarette in the other, she stared into a wine bottle covered in dripped candle wax. I put back the canvas and tin cans, sealed the boxes, and shut the closet door on what remained of Papa's life: blue and yellow paint dried on a palette knife, colors hardened onto a wooden palette, empty tins, crinkled photos, royal blue and teal spattered on drop cloths.

PAINTING LESSONS (1966)

In Mr. Smiley's garage old newspapers, oily rags and canvases lay scattered along the concrete floor. Even with the electric garage door slung open, the room reeked of linseed oil, turpentine and cigar smoke. It was the combination of the three that I later identified with the scent of creativity. A burnt orange ray of sunlight slanted through the dusty window, illuminating my canvas — half undone. A blue sky tinged with mauve and pinks awaited a muddy road, a few autumn trees and white clouds with slightly gold under-highlights.

Mr. Smiley stood in the middle of the concrete floor, his Cincinnati Reds baseball cap pulled down over his eyes, tufts of thin gray hair pushing out from under the band like bird wings. He sucked a soggy cigar, making little burping noises as he squinted at my canvas. I squinted too, because I thought that's what artists did. I wondered if I could ever finish it.

Though I wasn't sure I was an artist, I loved this world of cadmium yellow, cobalt blue, and white titanium in crescents under my fingernails. I squinted at the painting, wondering what it would take to get me to Arles with rolls of canvas under my arm and camel hair brushes jabbed coquettishly into a bun on top of my head. The image of it thrilled me momentarily, sent a spasm of delight down my spine, racing along my arm, jumping from elbow to hand, causing a jerk in my wrist. I twitched and the paintbrush flew from my hand, leaving a burnt umber splat along my canvas. Red silence pierced the room.

"Well," Mr. Smiley said at last, "You can't blend that in; so I guess a tree goes there."

GOING HOME

Nurses in pink uniforms displayed metal name tags pinned above their breasts. Gray old men lost inside sweat suits and pajamas sported electronic wrist bracelets. Shiny metal carts of applesauce and pureed sausage wheeled by. In padded chairs, old men vacant as televisions watched images flicker across their mental screens. Chins up, mouths open, they stared at the ceiling and watched as childhood's stray dogs or old girlfriends appeared, while some relative whose name they'd forgotten spooned scrambled eggs into their mouths.

I walked down the hall in the Alzheimer's wing of a nursing home for veterans. Papa's room sat all the way in the back, which meant I had to hold my breath for a very long time, past all the shit-reeking doorways. Old fellows wandered the hall, looking for places to lie down. The head-bangers wore padded contraptions resembling old-fashioned football helmets. Those still able to walk walked. They walked in and out of other people's rooms, uncertain where they belonged. They walked in sock feet, or with one shoe gone. They dribbled piss and feces and their pants hung if their diapers are full. Papa called them "The Space Invaders." I held my breath, and when I had to breathe, I breathed through my mouth the way an animal breathes when it is frightened.

"Where is my mother?" an old man called. He ran on socked tiptoes down the hall after me. "Where is my mother? Is she here yet?" Another touched my sleeve as I passed. His long fingernails scratched at the cloth of my shirt. He wanted to pet me, or to be petted. He leaned against me as I tried to scoot past him, dodging a violently yellow puddle in the hall. "Am I a dog?" he called softly.

I pushed open the door to Papa's room. He was asleep, his roommate out walking. Papa's head hung off the edge, his feet curled under him in fetal position. In his sleep he had grabbed the sheet like someone familiar that he had carried with him into his dream world, so he lay on a half-bare plastic mattress. The pillow was gone — probably stolen by a space invader. Papa's glasses had fallen on the floor. The room smelled like farts.

"Papa?" I called.

I hated to wake him, but I'd just driven seventy miles to see him, and I hadn't seen him in almost four weeks. None of my excuses could have meant anything to a man whose life revolved around waiting. I wanted to scream.

"Is it time to go home?" he asked.

"What?"

"They told me I can go home," Papa said.

"Who told you?"

"The doctor. He said I'm well now, and I can go home."

In a corner Papa had stacked all of his magazines, his Readers Digests, church bulletins and newspapers. On top of them lay a plastic sack of underwear and a tin of butterscotch candy. "I'm all packed," he said.

I sat in the pink vinyl chair beside the window. Big tears plopped onto the canvas bag I'd brought with me — a present of oil pastels and paper Papa would never use. He didn't see me slide the bag into the bottom of his dresser drawer next to the window. He was still all curled up and turned away.

A CLEAN SWEEP

Jane came from Colorado to visit the day I decided to quit smoking. That day I started cleaning to find some other frenzied motion for my empty hands besides covering my face and in-breathing sharply through my fingers, or tapping ink pens onto glass dishes. I swept under Jane's feet as she pieced together a quilt. "I can't imagine spending the rest of my life with a broom just to keep from smoking," I said.

"Have you thought about painting?"

A cloud of guilt clustered around me. Four years ago I'd wistfully mentioned to Doug that I once loved to paint, and for Christmas he bought me a canvas and a box of oils. I'd even gone out and bought myself a desk easel the following day at half-price. With the best of intentions, I put it all in the closet under the stairwell off the front porch and forgotten about it, except when I added the stainless steel paint box, palette, palette knife, crinkled tubes of paint and brushes that Papa had given me after I'd been taking painting lessons from Mr. Smiley all summer. Until that day I'd never known that Papa had been a painter. Later I found his art books, his books on calligraphy and drawing the human form, his teacher's watercolors and his college yearbook that read "Charles 'Slug' Davis, Art Club President." How odd that it had been my neighbor and not my father who had taught me to paint.

In that same closet I kept all of Mr. Smiley's arts supplies, too. When he moved from his house across the street and into an assisted living residence, he gave Mama his crushed tubes of oils, his variously shaped, and stained and well-used camel hair brushes with their pungent odor of linseed oils, paint, cigar smoke and turpentine.

I carried the broom upstairs to the little summer porch on the second floor of the house where Doug and I live. First, I swept cobwebs and dead lady bugs from the peeling wallpaper. Then, I set up the old iron bedstead with three mattresses and a chenille bedspread. I carried in a chair from the barn and covered it with an old blue drape, cleared the table, then arranged shelves of my father's art books that I had carried out of his basement.

On the wall I hung the portrait of my mother that Papa had painted after they were married: a dark-haired woman in a blue bathrobe, smoking a cigarette, one pale breast exposed, her hand draped around a cobalt blue coffee mug. With a little gasp of horror I noticed the thick blue paint from the coffee mug and the bathrobe had begun to chip. When I had carried this crumbling painting out of my father's closet in the basement I had asked my mother about it. She laughed saying, of course I could have the painting. She called it "The Blue Bitch." She didn't like it because it wasn't flattering.

    I sat on the bed on the summer porch on the second floor landing and stared at my father's painting, the only piece of art to survive rejection. As I sat on the bed looking at the lines, the colors, and the signature, my father sat seventy miles away in a nursing home where he could no longer even write his own name. Before me, on the table, a blank canvas waited on an easel by the window beside the oils and brushes — a blank canvas that was my father himself.

FIGHTING POVERTY

My father drives mountain back roads, across creek beds, alongside coal trucks, and in the dark through grey little towns that tilt toward the train tracks. The towns have funny names like Lick Skillet, and Mousie, Hell for Certain and Whoopflarea. They are filled with mayors, county executives and coal operators who don't really want my Daddy there. He drives the mountains sometimes with sacks full of clothes and 'learning' toys, but mostly with a head full of big ideas backed by federal money. We live in Frankfort, but he drives all over the mountains to go to work.

"Will you be gone all week?" I ask him.

If he is gone, Mama will be in one of her moods — smoking furiously, lecturing about religion incessantly, or sending me into the basement to iron blouses, pants and shirts. She had to quit her job because of me, because I am the child born in an odd year, which meant that when they closed the Negro schools and integrated us, there was not enough room for everyone to go to the same school together. My brothers go to school from 7 am until 1 pm; I go to school in the same building from 1 pm until 7pm. My mother left her nice job working for the governor's office to stay home and 'mother' me. She watches me like a hawk all day.

If I can't see my father or my brothers, I'd rather be ironing.

"Why do you have to be gone again?" I ask my father.

Because, he says, in one of those coal camps, up some hollow, or by some creek, there might be a child who is cold and hungry.

"Or lonesome," I say.

"That's right."

Daddy talks the mountain mothers into sending their children to one of his Head Start schools. He helps the community build playgrounds and brings round the public health nurses to give the babies their shots. He makes a point of getting things done that some people can't or won't do for themselves. That's why the mayors don't like him. He makes them look bad.

"You don't need an education to work in the mines," the mayor in Floyd County says.

"I don't want my baby to go to school," one Mama says. "She'll just get too smart and leave away from home. I don't want my boys going off to Detroit or Dayton and getting into trouble."

At a White House conference in 1964 Daddy received an award and shook hands with President Johnson who congratulated my father for being "a frontline lieutenant in the War on Poverty." My Daddy wants the children of coal miners to read, to flush their toilets, to drink milk from a bottle, and to live in houses with bedspreads and curtains. He hires young men and women to drive across creeks and up dirt roads to take the children to school, to give them their shots, to fix their teeth, and, yes, to show them a world beyond the mines.

"While you're chasing the pot of gold for people you don't even know," Mama complains, "what is it at the end of the day that we get out of it?"

My father's search for a better life for others has left my mother bitter. While I'm trying to write a social studies paper describing John Trumbull's portraits of the Creek Indians, Mama is arguing with herself and my absent father behind my back. "I thought when I got married," Mama says, "that'd I'd finally have a real family with a husband who comes home and puts his feet under the supper table every night. I didn't know I would be a single parent raising three children."

One spring Daddy went to Washington to meet the nation's congressmen and shake hands with President Johnson. My brothers, Mama, and I went along with him in his green Impala. While he was in meetings we toured the Capitol Building, the White House, the Lincoln Monument, the Smithsonian Institute, and the National Art Museum. My father thought we should see something educational and interesting. From behind the thick, smoky stench of the yellow curtains on the fifth floor of the Francis Scott Key hotel, my brothers and I peered out the rain-streaked window and down into the crowded street. We were hoping to see John, Paul, George, and Ringo step out of a cab. We complained to Mama that we didn't have tickets to see their concert. We knew The Beatles were in town because the hotel lobby was filled with memorabilia.

"I know your father is in town, too," Mama replied, puffing her cigarette and staring at the television, "but I don't get to see him."

Back home Daddy is still wooing legislators by driving with them through the mountains. They talk to miners, politicians, and moonshiners. Daddy puts his faith in his silver tongue and in the moonshine and the martini shakers, vodka, and vermouth inside the photographer's case that he has hidden in his car trunk. He used a Dymo Labelmaker to identify its contents. It reads "Poverty Kit."

Clear moonshine shimmers inside the water glasses in motel rooms along blue highways. My father's liquor funds his war on poverty. Late Friday nights he comes home carrying his garment bag up the sidewalk and into the house. Then he drives up to the Windmill Liquors on the corner "to pick up a little something" in a paper bag. If I am lucky enough to go with him, I get beer nuts in a red-striped tin foil bag. Late at night alone on the sofa in the living room, Daddy watches Johnny Carson, laughs, and eats sardines on Saltine crackers. His drink sweats inside its metal glass in the coaster on the coffee table.

The nights he does not come home I lie in bed, listening to one-sided phone conversations with Mama. "Tomorrow," she says, repeating him in a tired angry voice. "Tomorrow? Let me tell you where you can go right now."

Some nights when he comes home late, I listen to the sound of Mama breaking dishes. I think as hard as I can, shouting with my mind, "Don't do it, Mama! He'll just leave again!" But she has an angry cloud-roiling inside her so she doesn't hear me. Many weeks all I see of my Daddy is his back as he carries double-packed suitcases down the sidewalk, loads them into the trunk of his car, and drives away.

My father has worn out five cars going up and down mountain roads. He wrecked two of them. It's entirely possible he'd been drinking. I heard how the coal truck in Beattyville tore off the front end of his Pontiac; an inch closer and it would have torn off his legs. At night Mama makes us fold our hands and pray. We pray that Daddy will come home to stay. My little brother prays that Daddy won't lose his job and leave us homeless with no food to eat. He's heard about the mountain children living in cement block houses by the creeks with only a thin little stream of smoke coming out of their chimneys to make them warm.

"We've got a house," Mama says. "And food to eat."

"We've got Charles Chips in a can on the front porch," Alan adds. "And a good mother."

"And a good Daddy," I say.

Mama bites her lip. She's trying not to say it, but she says what we're thinking. "If he was so good why isn't he home with his wife and children instead of our running the countryside?"

While lying in bed kicking at covers because I can't sleep I listen to the Mama side of the conversation. Daddy really does call her every night. "I would think if you loved me that much, you'd want to be at home with me." There's a long silence. "Your children miss you. I think they've almost forgotten what you look like."

When Daddy comes home, he brings me a cedar coin box that is stamped in gold across the top. It reads: "Natural Bridge State

FIGHTING POVERTY

Park, Slade, Kentucky." I put it on my bookshelf along with the other cedar boxes in my collection. They are all stuffed with money. Quarters go in the Pine Mountain State Park box, nickels and dimes in the Cumberland Falls, copper pennies in the Springfield, Kentucky box, Boyhood Home of Abraham Lincoln. "Put a dollar in the box," I tell Daddy.

"What's that for?" he asks.

"That's to buy us a new car for whenever you wear out or wreck this one."

"I can see your mother's been giving you her lectures again."

"That okay," I say. "She says you and me don't pay her any attention, anyway."

In the summer I ride along with Daddy to his meetings in Hazard, Jackson, Prestonsburg, or Manchester. Sometimes he takes bags filled with clothes, or checks, or music LPs and art supplies to the child care centers. I like to repeat the names of the town through which we pass: Blackey, Greasy Creek, Buckhorn, and Hindman. The flabby-armed cooks at the centers squeal and jiggle when they see Daddy coming up the sidewalk. They lay aside special plates of cornbread and butter just for him. He rolls up his sleeves to eat.

It's summer and I'm with my father, so I don't mind waiting. I'm learning to do it well. In Isom I sit in a tire swing, spinning in circles, and I wait. In Vicco two little girls and I make crayon rubbings of burr oak leaves. In Wheelwright, a strange, narrow, soot-covered town, I sleep in the front seat of Daddy's Pontiac with the windows rolled down. The sun sets early in the mountains as I wait for him to finish his tediously long community center meeting.

I don't get to stay overnight, but one night I got to hear Daddy tell his office workers and some state legislators about his adventures. After he's written the checks and the centers close, he might accept a supper invitation at one of his staff workers' houses. Once after a meal, he sat in a wooden porch swing with the 90-year-old matriarch — his employee's great grandmother. They listened to her sons, Cyrus and Bill, play the fiddle and banjo, while Bill's wife and daughter clogged on the porch.

"Mr. Davis," the old woman asked him, "Do ye pick?"

No, he said, he didn't pick. "I never was too musically inclined."

She rocked a minute, thinking. Then she said, "Do ye dance?"

"Oh, I don't dance anymore," Daddy said. "My knees have given out on me."

She rocked a little more, thinking. "Well, do ye sing?"

Daddy laughed. "Oh well, I can't carry a tune."

The old woman grunted and looked up at my father with pity. "Well," she finally mumbled. "Ye don't do much, do ye."

When Daddy tells that story he laughs and rattles the metal shakers in which he has mixed a very dry martini for one of the legislators. Their office aides laugh with him. He and Mama are entertaining Daddy's board members in the living room. It's Christmas. There's a fire in the grate and mistletoe hung over all the doorways in the house. Bing Crosby is crooning about being home for Christmas and Daddy is singing along. We've decorated the house with bright little sofa throws to hide the worn places in the couch. Mama's wearing a beautiful green brocade sheath that she made from discount draperies from her brother's home furnishing shop. She looks like a million bucks, but she's got her red lips pursed and keeps tapping her wedding ring in irritation against the metal tumbler of vodka in her hand. It sounds like someone beating a metal pipe with a wrench.

Daddy gives her a look. She gives him one back.

"No, I don't do much," he says, repeating the punch line of his little joke. "I don't do much at all." He gives the tumbler one last shake and pours the concoction into his state representative's glass. In the golden firelight Mama's eyes snap with their own kind of smouldering fire while the ice chips in the legislator's glass glitter like money.

TWO MORE OF THE SAME

Ed and Ray are two friends who work together at the bomb factory. Ray wears Roy Orbison hair, cowboy boots with steel heels, and jeans. His eight hairy knuckles advertise two emotions. His Camel straights ride proud and square and tight in the breast pocket of his green tee-shirt. Ray spends his morning with a tiny screwdriver, tightening the ends of 140 fuse boxes. He is making some very big bombs for his country.

Ed wears gray slacks, a tie, and a white lab coat with his name on it. He keeps the cuffs of his white shirt buttoned down. He comes around with a clipboard to see Ray several times a day and to make sure that the fuse boxes are tight. Sometimes he tells Ray to take the screws out and tighten them down again, but that's his job, and it doesn't bother Ray. Every now and then Ed says, "We shipped 20,000 'end-items' this week." And Ray understands. They hardly talk about the bombs.

In the cafeteria, Ed and Ray set their pails on a Formica table, then open them to look inside. Ed makes his own lunch every morning — two peanut butter sandwiches and an apple. He is not married. Ray's wife re-invents things from leftovers, like barbecued chicken salad or meat loaf sandwiches. Today he has leftover lasagna and he pops it in the microwave.

"I wish I had a beer with this," says Ray.

"Yeah, me too. You wanna go for a beer again tonight?"

"What the hell," says Ray and slaps Ed's back. "There ain't nothing like a tall, cold one."

After work the friends meet at Ed's car. He has a metallic blue Pontiac Firebird with imitation lambskin seat covers and a great sound system. A pink and white garter hangs from the rear-view mirror. He is not married.

Ray drives a station wagon with collie hairs and a four-day old shitty diaper in the back. The floor just behind the driver's seat is full of McDonald's paper bags and Styrofoam burger caddies. His car is parked next to Ed's. Before Ray leaps into Ed's passenger seat, he looks inside his own car and sees the dirty diaper. He thinks, by the time I get home the baby will be asleep. He remembers his wife said the baby had two new teeth. He forgot to look in its mouth this morning.

Ed pulls out of the parking lot, reaches behind him into the paper sack on the floor, and pulls out two tall, cold ones. He shoves a CD into the crevice of his dashboard. He likes to drive fast and wink at girls in Toyotas.

"Where'd you get this?" asks Ray.

"I went to a drive-up window at break. You like Hamm's, don't you?"

"Never anything but," Ray says.

"Yeah, me too. Nothing like a Hamm's after work," says Ed.

"Nothing like it," Ray agrees.

Ed slides the car into a parking place between two Toyotas in front of the Broken Drum. Ed searches the room for a table. Ray glances along the sticky wooden bar for two empty stools. They take a Naugahyde booth near the front so they can watch girls coming in. The booth is torn at the corner behind Ed's head. Ed orders a Hamm's. Ray falters, orders a Bud.

The bottles of liquor and the rows of faces are amplified in the bar-room mirror. Ray glimpses Joe Daily on a stool at the bar. He drinks from his bottle without tipping his head back. He stares straight into the mirror. Ray watches Joe Daily drink. He sees the side of Ed's face, then recognizes his own. When Ray drinks, he tips his bottle up just like Joe Daily. The first beers go down fast.

"There's Joe Daily from work," Ed says.

"Uh-huh."

"He's drinking by himself again."

Ray looks again as Joe Daily stares at himself in the mirror. Joe's reflection smokes a cigarette and rakes its hand through his hair. He mixes big vats of potassium nitrate and sulfur in a different building from Ed and Ray. He has six kids and lives in the San Lorenzo trailer park. He's missing two of his fingers. He snuffs out his cigarette as Ray lights his. Their eyes meet each other's within the mirror.

"Should we ask him over?"

"Naw," says Ray. "He's married. He probably likes to drink alone."

Joe Daily shakes himself, stops staring in the mirror and gulps down the beer in front of him. The door slams as he leaves.

Ed glances over his shoulder at the retreating Joe and thinks, He's probably going home now. He'll probably give the kids a bubble bath and eat a big dinner with lots of vegetables. His wife will rub his neck.

He'll probably take out the garbage, watch a little TV, and knock back another beer before bed, Ray thinks. That's what Ray always does. He says goodnight and kisses his wife's shoulder, then she rolls away. That's what happens to guys like Joe and Ray.

The blond young waitress stands by the table with a wet rag slung across her forearm. She wears a turquoise tee-shirt silk-screened with mountains that advertise Boulder. Her breasts give added dimensions to Long's Peak. Ray would like to lie down on that peak. He wouldn't even mind if he froze to death.

"Again?" she asks, lifting their bottles.

The two friends nod. She turns away, but not until she mumbles to Ed, "Nice car." Ed scowls and turns away.

Ray mumbles to her back, "Nice ass."

"Life's a piece of shit, Ray," Ed says. "I'd like to quit the bomb factory. I don't like to think of myself killing little kids."

"I don't think about it," says Ray.

"I'd like to go to California or Nebraska or somewhere. I'd like to have meaningful relationships."

"I'd like a Pontiac Firebird," says Ray.

"But I probably won't. Quit the factory, I mean."

"Me neither, but I'd still like a Pontiac Firebird, so girls in Toyotas would wink at me."

"It's a nice car," Ed agrees.

The sun sets while the two friends sit drinking beer. Ed lines up all his empty Hamm's bottles so that he can count them. He watches the last rays of sunlight filter through the six amber bottles and thinks about the shadows out on the plains. He wants to get in his car and drive out there. He's always wondered where it was east of him that the shadows of the mountain begin to overtake the shadows of the evening. He wants to stand at that intersection just for the instant that the sun disappears. He wants to stand drunk and swaying a little in the last light, and feel it on his face. Then when the light disappears, he wants to go away with it.

"I'll have another beer," Ed tells the waitress.

"I'll have the same," says Ray.

"Hamm's?" says the waitress.

"No," Ray says. "The same. The usual. As in 'another of the same like the other.'" He turns his bottle so that she can read the label.

"How many dead soldiers you got?" asks Ed. He lines up Ray's beer bottles for him. There are five, eleven now in all: six in front of Ed and five in front of Ray. The waitress picks up all the beer bottles, shakes the rag from her arm, and wipes the table. There are no more bottles in front of Ed and Ray.

Ray looks around the room. It is filled with a gray cigarette haze, a grimness that makes all the men and the bottles in the bar look the same dim color. He glances in the barroom mirror and thinks he sees Joe Daily again, talking to someone, but it's not Joe Daily. It is Ray himself, talking to the waitress.

"Any what?" he asks.

"Hors d'oeuvres. You know, food. Aren't you hungry? Do you want something to eat?"

"No thanks," says Ray.

He looks at his watch. It's past dinner time. Probably his wife has already put the leftover meat in the oven and left it warming. The meat will be dry when he gets there. Whenever he and Ed drink beer after work, she leaves the oven on a little too high so that his meat dries out.

"I'll have a burger," Ed says, "with onions."

"I'll have the same," says Ray.

"Another beer?" asks the waitress.

"No, the same," Ray says. "I'll have a burger — the same thing Ed is having."

"And another beer," Ed says.

"Yeah, me too. What the hell. Two more of the same. There's nothing like a tall, cold one after a long, hard one."

"Day," Ed says.

The waitress turns away, walks to the next table where two girls have seated themselves. They glance at Ed and Ray, then giggle. Ed sees that they are very young girls. They wear their red halters as tight as apple skins. They look back at him, avert their eyes, and twitter.

Ed admires the waitress's beautiful legs, then glances at her sensible brown shoes. He wonders if anyone will love him. He feels old. His hair grays at the temples. He wouldn't want a young girl to mother his baby. Girls get younger and prettier all the time, he thinks. They're no longer interesting. He'd like a sensible woman who had some gray in her hair.

The waitress takes the girls' orders and crosses to the bar. For the first time, Ed looks into her face. Her front teeth overlap slightly, just enough to make her interesting. She brings back two beers to their table, then turns smoothly, scoops up the bottles on the vacant table beside them, dumps them in the barrel by the end of the bar, and surveys the room briefly before resting her hip on the end bar stool and lighting a cigarette. Ed and Ray watch her smoke.

"You think she's pretty?" asks Ed.

"I wouldn't kick her outta bed."

"D'you see her teeth?"

"Yeah, teeth. What about 'em?"

Ray sips his beer, thinking he should have looked in the baby's mouth this morning.

"They're crooked. Not a little, but a lot."

"I was looking at her ass," says Ray.

"I think that's why she smokes out of the corner of her mouth," says Ed.

When the burgers come, Ed and Ray eat in silence. Ed adds ketchup to his, takes a bite, and squeezes at the same time. The ketchup oozes out one side. Ray wishes he'd come to the Broken Drum alone like Joe Daily. He could drink one beer and go home. In the middle of his burger he wants to go home and look in the baby's mouth. When he does go, his wife won't say mean things. Secretly, she'll be mad and blame Ray's drinking on Ed, but she won't say anything. She grinds her teeth in her sleep.

Ed lines up five more empty beer bottles on the table and orders himself another. The waitress asks the two friends to pay up; she's getting ready to go home. She wipes the table. Ed grabs her hand and holds its flattened, slightly damp palm to his heart. He asks the waitress to take him home with her. Ray looks at his beer bottle and begins to scrape off the label with his nails. He mutters, declaring that he will take Ed out to the car, then jam his fingers down Ed's throat, all the way up to his knuckles that spell L-O-V-E.

Ed kicks Ray under the table and slaps the beer out of Ray's hand. "You son of a bitch," he shouts. "What've I got to lose?"

"Your beer," says Ray.

"Take me home," Ed begs the waitress.

He's always wanted a sensible woman, but he's had pretty girls instead. Pretty girls make him lie; they make him say things he doesn't mean. They bore him and he gets angry. He calls them sluts so that they will go away. If they don't go away, he has to get meaner.

"I'm not really mean," he tells the waitress. "I'm lonely."

He wants to go home with her or she can go home with him. It really doesn't matter. It's only for the night, if that's okay with her, just the night, or if she wants something else they could work it out in the morning.

"Just don't make me lie," he says.

All he wants is to watch her in the kitchen cooking breakfast, breaking eggs just for him.

The waitress looks at Ed, then Ray, then sighs. The Long's Peak of her tee-shirt heaves as if her heart were breaking at the mountain's dark core. "I'm married," she says. "But I'll take you home — to your home — because you're drunk. But that's all. Believe me, I'm really sorry; but that's all."

Across the table, Ed slides his car keys toward Ray.

A new waitress comes around to Ray's table with a rag slung over her arm. She's sixty at least, with dried up dyed black hair. The coral lipstick of her mouth has worked itself onto her teeth. Ray orders another beer. The girls at the next table order another round and the waitress asks for their identification. The girls sling their purses over their shoulders and head for the door. They stop on the way to shoot a game of pinball. They're not very good, so it doesn't take long. Over the noise of Johnny Paycheck on the jukebox, Ray hears the lethargic thump of the ball hitting a flipper arm before it slips down the hole.

Ray's sure that by now his wife is asleep. When he married her she was so pretty that he couldn't wait to wake up in the morning. Now he sleeps with his face turned away. She grows old. She sags. Her breasts are two heavy milk pitchers she's always emptying for the children. The first thing she does when she wakes up is stiffen and slam her eyes tight again. We used her up, thinks Ray. Some mornings he watches her get up and he counts the lines in her face. He hasn't told her this, but he watches. He sips his beer and wonders if she misses him while she's asleep.

Whenever she's at the grocery too long Ray wonders if she'll come back. He imagines a yellow station wagon hitting her in the grocery parking lot. He can see her lying on the pavement with blood flowing out of her ear and bright oranges and fat, green artichokes rolling out of the paper bag. He imagines the same scene over and over, but it's impossible to tell if he's afraid of it or wishing for it.

She left him once for six days. He spent the first two nights drinking beer and playing cards with the boys from work. Then the baby rolled off the edge of the bed. He'd been changing the baby's diapers when someone said to hurry up and play, it was his turn. He left the baby on the bed. It was only a minute, but the baby rolled off and hit its head on the linoleum floor. It cried and he couldn't comfort it. One of its eyes drifted in toward its nose. He was afraid he'd made the baby stupid. He made everyone leave. "Just take your money and leave," he'd said. The baby fell asleep, crying in his arms.

It woke up screaming again in the middle of the night and Ray sat up until sunrise rocking it. He promised that would never happen again, if God would only make the baby all right. He was its father. He loved the baby. Its crying was breaking his heart.

In the morning the baby's eye was fine. She was only crying now because she was hungry. There was a small blue and green ring about the size of a quarter on her otherwise perfect, porcelain white head. The bump didn't seem to bother the baby, but it made him sick to look at it. When his wife came back four days later, there were no words between them. She never told Ray why she left or why she came back. He was glad she came back then, but he never told her. And he never told her about the baby.

"You going to nurse that thing or kill it?"

Ray looks up and sees the old waitress pointing at his beer. She has a fistful of empty bottles and points at his. There aren't many people left in the bar. They must've all found somebody to go home with.

"Kill it," Ray says and kills it.

She wipes the table with her rag. He ought to go home now, Ray thinks, and tell his wife about the baby. He should tell her he still loves her, at least at times. He should tiptoe into the baby's room and watch it breathe. The baby would look warm and sweet in its blankets.

"What'll it be?" asks the waitress. "Another?"

Ray puts Ed's car keys in his pocket. He sees himself in the barroom mirror. There's no one around — no one at all, just the two Rays: the one in the booth and the one in the mirror. They blow smoke at each other. They drink their beers.

I want ... I want ... The Ray in the mirror is thinking. The barroom lights explode momentarily like sunrise after a long, lonesome, stretch on a darkened highway.

"Decide, honey. We're closing in five."

"Yeah, another," Ray says, and then gestures toward the bar. "And one for my friend there."

Tonight he could drive that Pontiac Firebird all the way to Phoenix.

SPIRITUALISM

Mama died thirteen weeks ago on Friday. All her life she'd been robust, but by the time she died she'd wasted down to bones — all because that midget only fed her peas and rice. Everything else clogged up her chakras. That's what the midget said. If it weren't for her blue hair and fat woman's clothes, I'd have hardly recognized my ghost as Mama. The fact is I was haunted. She appeared twice daily at 5:05 and smacked me hard on the head. Last Thursday she hit me such a clap she sent my glasses flying and caused my ears to ring. For such a little bitty thing, she held a powerful grudge.

I remember how it started a year ago last April after Daddy died of split intestines. I was sitting in the glider on the sun porch, watching Mama prune begonias, when all of a sudden her face glazed over like a doughnut and this sugary film settled on top of her. Her scissors paused above an angel-wing begonia as she watched a shiny, blue-green fly rattle against the glass.

"People's souls are like that," Mama said. "Always trying to get out, but the minute they do, trying to find a little hole to sneak back in."

She snipped her scissors beheading a geranium.

I let it pass like most things Mama said. Then about two weeks later when I woke thirsty in the night, I found Mama in the living room talking to the television. She'd propped her feet in the Lazy Boy and there, in her pink nightie with the fuzzy pom-pom slippers, she was chatting it up with Daddy.

"Alden, it's so good to see you," she said. She moved up close to the television screen. Blue light flooded the room, elongating the shadows of the dieffenbachia. In the electronic glow, Mama herself seemed iridescent. "You look a might thin, darling. What're they feeding you yonder?"

I tiptoed up behind and peered over her shoulder. Nothing on the screen but noise and snow. I crawled off to bed, resolved that in the morning I would nip this little problem in the bud.

"Mama," I said.

She was scrubbing egg off the fork tines.

"Now that Daddy's gone, I must look after you. And I'm thinking I ought to take you to the MD, since you ain't been in some time."

She threw the forks in the sink. "Don't spy on me, Charlotte Rose," she said. "I knowed you was there. I felt you breathing on me the whole time. Leave alone what you don't understand."

"I'm sure I don't know what you mean," said I.

Mama shook her crooked finger. "I'm not crazy, Charlotte."

I left it alone two weeks, but it didn't get any better. Mama started listening to one of those afternoon dial-a-psychic radio shows sponsored by the herbal tea people. It featured the Reverend Spoon — a whiney nose-talker if I ever heard one — who'd tell folks to sleep with their heads pointed north and their feet south, things like that, if they wanted to dream about the future. Of course, I didn't pay it much mind, but Mama rearranged furniture.

She still talked all night to the television, discussing it all from animism to bunions, but she never felt obliged to tell me about it. I'll venture because she knew I wouldn't listen. Every morning I'd find her passed out in the Lazy Boy, TV blaring. I'd just turn it off and make toast. I didn't like it, but I could have lived with it. She was my mother, after all. If only that midget hadn't come.

One afternoon I was golden-frying chicken when the doorbell rang. I opened the door, and there he stood not more than three-

and-a-half feet high, with at least two feet of ponytail hanging down. He grinned up with his little bitty corncob teeth.

"I've come about Alden," he said.

"Mr. Davis is no longer with us," I said. "He passed away nine weeks ago."

The midget squinted his eyes and laughed. It was more like a wheeze really. His chest heaved and his tongue passed in and out of his teeth.

"I don't see a thing funny about it," I said.

He smiled like a television evangelist. "I was called. Someone at this address called yesterday. The Reverend Spoon sent me."

That's when I slammed the door.

"Who was that?" Mama asked.

"Girl Scout cookies," I said, and went back to frying chicken.

A few nights later I was painting my toenails and Mama was watching Wild Kingdom when the midget strolled right into our living room. He pulled up a kitchen chair and plunked down in front of the television, with his red tennis shoes wrapped around the chair legs. I upset the nail polish on the carpet.

"Don't he look comfortable?" said I.

He took a fat hand from his jacket pocket and gave it to Mama. "I'm Wade," he said.

"Alma," she said. "That there's Charlotte Rose. She don't believe in anything."

"I know," he said. "We've met." He turned and stared at the television. "What time's he come on?"

"After Johnny Carson," Mama said. "He knows how I love Johnny Carson."

"You act like you know this man," I said.

"The Reverend said to expect him. We're going to church now, Charlotte. Don't wait up."

If you think I'd let Mama run off with a midget, think again. I tore out the tissue between my toes and — wet toenails and all — stuffed my feet down in some shoes. All right, it was rash of me, but I figured a little church couldn't hurt her. Maybe it'd put the fear of God in her and she'd forget all this foolishness. Leastwise, I figured they might convince her to stop watching television all night, even if she did sleep with her head pointed north.

Imagine my surprise to find the Center of Divine Thought housed in the basement of the public library. We had to walk single-file through a catacomb of musty newspapers to reach the auditorium. Somebody was already there setting up folding chairs when the band strolled in carrying guitars, mandolins, and an upright bass.

"Exactly what is it your church believes?" I asked Wade.

"Everything," he said. "We believe it's all possible."

When the band struck up, Mama and I found back row seats. The congregation rose and sang, and Wade slammed his tambourine. Up front, a grown man with thinning hair clacked away on some kitchen spoons. When the song stopped, he stepped to the podium.

"I'm the Reverend Spoon," he said, his lips twisting around a scar. His eyes seemed amazed as two June bugs squashed on his glasses. "Brothers and Sisters," he said smiling. He tipped his head side to side. "Children of the Light, I don't need the money, but the landlord likes to see it. So empty your pockets at the door."

Wade shook the tambourine and beat it — bam, bam, bam. Then the service started.

We should've left right then. That was the strangest bunch I ever saw. Some tax consultant from Peytona jumped up on his chair and said he'd been abducted by aliens from the Triangulum Nebulae. "There are over two billion inhabited planets in the universe, each with its own presiding god," he said. "Except ours, which has a multitude — creations of our confused minds."

He said some other things I didn't listen to and thumped a book he'd written about it. When he finished, everybody fell quiet. Then a red-haired woman in a jumpsuit sprang up, shouting, "I believe it."

And everybody shouted, "I believe it!"

She told how she'd been snatched off Big Sandy Mountain by aliens and zapped back down into a Chicago phone booth. The phone was ringing. It was one of God's angels.

And everybody shouted, "I believe it!"

Then a fat man fell into the aisle, his eyes rolled back, and his mouth filled with foam. He pounded the floor with his fists, beating out the message of angels in African drum language. Wade banged his tambourine, and I said, "Let's get the hell out of here," but Mama sat wide-eyed and muttered under her breath, "I believe it."

And everybody shouted.

Before I could stop her, she up and said she'd seen Daddy on TV. Well, nobody said anything. It was so quiet that you could've heard my jaw drop. And she just stood there looking the fool. I grabbed her sleeve and made her sit.

"Let's go," I said and took her elbow.

She jerked free, raised up, crossed her hands over her shiny pocketbook, and said louder this time. "He's been dead ten weeks, and I see him every night. Comes on right after Johnny Carson. We just talk mostly. He says things like: 'I miss you, Alma, honey.' and 'Didn't we have a good time at Mammoth Cave that Sunday in 1945?' and 'Jesus Christ lives in this TV set with me.' Last week he had lunch with Mahatma Gandhi. Tuna salad, he said."

The midget jumped on his chair, swinging his arms around. "I believe it!" he shouted and smashed his tambourine. The Reverend clicked his spoons and said, "I believe it!" Everybody jumped up shouting. I just put my face in my hands.

Mama sniffed and pointed at me. "She don't. She don't believe nothing. Thinks I'm crazy. Her own Daddy and she don't believe it. She don't even say hello to him."

"Mama!" I shouted.

Everybody stared, then they rose all at once and came at me. "Believe it! Believe it!" they shouted.

Guitars played. Tambourines shook. People squeezed in all around, putting their hands on me, buzzing in my ears. I swung my pocketbook, beating them off like horseflies. I never ran so fast in my life and didn't look up until I got home, crawled into bed, and pulled the covers over my head. But who could sleep after something like that?

Around midnight Mama came in, flipped on the kitchen light, got a cold beer, and then went in the living room to talk to the TV. I can imagine what she said. The next morning I snapped off the television and made toast like nothing happened, but Mama'd stopped speaking. I let her do as she pleased. Sooner or later, I thought, it'd pass.

At breakfast I said, "Mama, let's you and me go to Mammoth Cave. We could have some fun."

She sniffed, took her fork, and scraped the scrambled eggs I'd fixed into the garbage.

That's how things went from bad to worse. Before I knew it, that midget was showing up every night, drinking our beer and watching TV, staying up all night. He drew an alphabet with magic marker on the new oilcloth of my kitchen table and started contacting demons with an upturned water glass. I'd wake up and find them both passed out in front of the television — Mama in her Lazy Boy and the midget on the floor, his head resting on her knees. I'd kick him out, but he'd be back before supper, and pretty soon he started staying for breakfast.

I tried talking it out. "Mama," I said, "you cannot contact spirits with a water glass and Daddy is not on TV. I don't believe any of it, except that you're being made the fool."

"That's possible," she said.

"You done taken in that hooey and turned your back on God."

"I'll take my God over yours," she said. "Mine's got more imagination."

I knew it wouldn't do to argue. I spun on my heel and walked. That afternoon I found my two suitcases on the front porch, so I picked them up and left. But I couldn't put the past behind me. I felt the devil closing in. I loved Mama, and I wasn't going to let him have her, though I knew she'd been turned against me. I had to take the situation in hand. And that's what I did. I spent three sleepless nights at the Days Inn just thinking about it.

As God is my witness, I didn't mean to harm a soul, but I'd reached my wit's end. That third night I crept home with a sledgehammer and peeped in the living room window. There they were stretched out on the leather sofa and in the Lazy Boy, watching Johnny Carson. There was Hostess cupcake wrappers strewn everywhere.

"There's Alden!" shouted Mama, pointing to the space right of Ed McMahon's fat ear. "Turn down the sound so we can hear."

Wade jumped off the sofa and adjusted the rabbit ears. The picture was already mostly fuzz and snow. Only the dim outline of figures danced across the screen.

"That's better," he said.

"Alden, honey!" Mama cried. "Say something."

They held hands and swayed in front of the television. It made me sick to see it. Then they fell quiet, listening to the static of the vacant screen. That's when I slipped in.

"He ain't saying nothing. Oh, look! He's fading now. He's waving goodbye," Mama cried. "Alden, come back, honey! Oh, me! He's been called to a place beyond."

She slumped down in the Lazy Boy and let Wade rub her head. That's when I raised my hammer and ran. I tell you a definite look of surprise crossed their faces. Even now I see their eyes widening, their jaws falling, their mouths turning into round O's. As I leveled the sledgehammer into the TV, a blast of light rose out of my hands. Sparks and glass flew. Smoke rolled out like I'd opened the gates of hell, and a jolt of lightning passed through me. Wade fell back and Mama rose slowly from her Lazy Boy, tiptoeing around the shards of glass. Without a howdy-do, where-ya-been, or kiss-my-foot, she put on her green nubby coat and walked out the door.

For some time I did not see her, but Wade stayed on, eating my breakfasts, wringing his little hands, and staring at the remains of the television. Then one Sunday in the cold and drizzle, Mama struggled onto the front lawn and collapsed. I went out and picked her up. She was limp and thin as a noodle, must have been walking for days. I carried her to bed and tried feeding her, but she wouldn't eat. I bathed her, I sat with her, I talked to her. She just stared through me like I was vapor.

"Where's Wade?" she asked.

I threw up my hands and called in the midget. He sat with her day and night, putting his little cockroach arm around her and sniffing her cotton candy hair. Now that the television was broken, he spent all night at my kitchen table, receiving messages with a water glass.

"Peas and rice. It says to fix her peas and rice."

Breakfast, lunch, and dinner. I fixed peas and rice. Mama shriveled down to nothing before my eyes, and there wasn't a thing I could do. Her eyes sunk back in her head. Her teeth grew a green slime. The cuffs of her nightdress looked like she'd blown her nose on both sleeves. The midget sat rubbing her hand and drinking our beer. I must have trucked in a case of it. The bottles lined the windowsill along Mama's bed. That midget drank like a three-hundred pound man.

One afternoon he came in with a broken black-and-white television he'd found at a garage sale. You couldn't get a channel on it, but he rolled it up to her bedside and raised Mama's pillows high enough so that she could see. Thereafter, every time anybody crossed in front of the television set, Mama wheezed and gagged on her sputum. She made us leave it on all the time. I couldn't refuse a dying woman's request. She'd lie there all day and whimper, "Alden? Alden?" She was going from bad to worse.

Both of us sat with her, me on one side and Wade on the other. He bawled like a baby and rubbed her hand. It was dry and white as paper.

"Mama, you're dying," I said.

"I believe it," she said.

"Don't you want a priest, a minister, a doctor, something?"

She gagged and choked and wheezed. "Turn on the TV," she said.

"It's on," said Wade.

"I can't hear it. Turn on the TV."

Wade rolled the broken television closer and cranked up the volume. The static blasted so loud it like to plastered me to the wall.

"Alden?" Mama gasped. "Is that you?"

"He's in the TV," said the midget. "Just let yourself go into the TV. Release your soul to the void in Jesus."

She said something to the midget I couldn't hear.

"Turn it off!" I shouted.

"I'm gone," she said. "I'll see you."

Then she coughed and rattled and rolled her eyes, while Wade commended her spirit to the broadcast airwaves. Such an indecent way to die. It was all I could do to snap off the television set while the midget closed her eyes.

That was four months ago. I fixed Mama a beautiful grave next to Daddy's with both their names on a bronzed marker, but she did not stay in it. Some nights I'd see her slumped in the Lazy Boy or poised over her begonias. Other times she appeared in the corner of the room in a kind of blue TV glow. I had a priest throw holy water on the doorways, though I am a Methodist. I lit candles in churches all over town. I erected two stone angels by her grave to point the way to heaven. I knelt down with my lips in the dirt and begged her not to haunt me. But no matter where I was, like clockwork, at 5:05 she'd come by and smack me hard on the head.

SPIRITUALISM

Desperate, I called the midget. "You got to help me," I said. "You got to make Mama stay in her grave. My head is ringing like a bell."

He gave me his corncob smile and said, "There's a price."

"Anything," I said. "Just do it."

He smiled again. "I know just what she wants, too."

The morning that I woke clear-headed I couldn't believe it. It was the first time in weeks my skull hadn't hurt. I went to Mama's grave ready to get down on my knees and thank her, but nothing could have prepared me for the shock. There stood the midget, chisel in hand, tap-tapping on a huge slab of stone. He stepped back to read the message. My heart flew like a blackbird out of my chest. There was no name on the marker anywhere. No day born or died, no lilies, no Rest in Peace or Asleep in Jesus, just this stone television with letters three inches high that read: Thanks for Watching and Good Night.

"My God," I shouted. "Take it down."

"You'd rather get knocked in the head?"

I walked back down the hill. When it comes right down to it, I'm a selfish woman. I miss Mama, but I don't visit her grave with flowers. The fact is I don't go much of anywhere. The house is quiet now and I like that. No television, no phone, no midget, just me and the silence of my begonias, and oh, once in a while, maybe the buzz of a fly somewhere, trapped in the house and rattling against the glass.

REAL ESTATE

On the Sunday before Thanksgiving Mama called all three of her children saying she wanted to talk. I cradled the earpiece against my shoulder and continued ironing, knowing that in about ten minutes, whether or not the choir robe was pressed, I'd have to hustle my daughter to church to sing. So far, she hadn't even taken a shower. Glaring, I snapped my fingers at Helene, who sat at the kitchen table dawdling over a bowl of Cocoa Puffs.

"I have things I need to say," Mama said.

"Okay," I told her. "I'm listening."

"We have to talk as a family."

"Okay," I said, "Talk to me. What do you want to talk about?"

"We'll talk about it later," Mama said. Then she arranged for me to meet her at her house on Thanksgiving. "Only I'm not going to cook a turkey dinner. I just want to talk. Your brother is coming with the turkey."

I promised to bring a broccoli casserole and dessert.

On Tuesday evening while the student papers I was grading flowed over my lap and cascaded across the sofa, my brother called. I motioned for Helene to turn down the TV; she blinked at me as if I were speaking Chinese. I got up to turn down the television and papers spilled from my lap onto the floor. With the red ink pen clenched between my teeth, I sorted papers while I talked with my brother.

"Say that again?" I said.

"I said," he said. (I could almost see his eyebrows furrowing) "What's this meeting about on Thursday at Mother's?"

"I don't know," I answered, circling a comma splice I had missed before. "Thanksgiving, I guess. I thought we were going to eat dinner. I said I'd bring the dessert...."

"She's got this meeting planned," he interrupted.

"I know," I said, circling a student's third run-on sentence.

"But she won't say what it's about."

I could almost hear a red sizzle rising up from his chest to his neck. My brother didn't like surprises. Our mother was often full of surprises. A few months before, she had surprised us by rescuing a South African woman and letting her live in the basement. The woman spoke very little English, but she had made it clear that her husband was trying to beat her. So Mama assured the woman that she could live in her basement "for a while." The woman had been living there for nearly a month when Mama had finally called that particular family meeting.

Because the woman could not pay rent, she had taken to doing Mama's ironing. This became the source of Mama's problem. The woman in her basement cried all day long, standing over the ironing board and making strange high-pitched shrieking sounds. Mama, of course, had called all three of her children and requested an immediate family meeting to discuss a resolution to this problem.

Our problem was that my brothers and I — all three of us — lived in different cities than Mama.

It usually took a crisis, a big secret and a family meeting to get us all in the same room solving Mama's problems together. Usually, however, she didn't like our solutions. Often she'd accuse me of taking sides with my father. My father didn't actually have to say anything for her to make this accusation.

As for the weeping woman in the basement, my brother had cancelled the family meeting and called the women's shelter.

"She's jerking us around is what she's doing," he said.

"Well, maybe she's just being dramatic," I answered "She's waiting for someone to make her life into a movie."

"This happens over and over," he said, his voice rising in volume. I held the phone at arm's length; and, in response, Helene turned up the television. "Every time she changes her mind, we've had to change our plans. This was our year to go to Indiana. Sheila's mother is not well...."

I wished that it was my year to go away somewhere. I wished I could drive up and down the knobs along Pea Ridge Road, looking at all the cars parked under the oak trees in front of somebody else's house. I wanted to ride along the ridges staring at clouds that looked like they were going to drop a foot of snow. Except the TV weatherman assured us that Thursday would be a gorgeous 72 degrees — perfect for a round of golf after turkey.

And I wasn't married, and I had nowhere else to go except to the house where I'd grown up.

"Do you know what she's got planned?" I asked.

"Hell, no," he said.

"I don't know why she won't just tell us what she's planning."

"Oh, it's a big surprise," he answered. "I hope it's not anything as stupid as last time."

While Danny detailed the vanishing plans he and Sheila had for the weekend, I found myself thinking about the time that I had come home from Colorado for a visit. Mama and Papa had taken Helene and me on a slow drive through the cemetery, all the while, Mama commented on the light through the cedars and the view overlooking the river. Papa had packed a picnic lunch with pimento cheese sandwiches, olives, and all of the accoutrements for his martinis — gin, vermouth, crushed ice, shot glasses, and shakers. They wanted to show me the cemetery plot they had recently purchased.

The whole thing was creepy enough that I was afraid somebody was sick.

Recalling this incident now made me wonder aloud to my brother, "You don't think one of them is sick, do you?" It was the kind of thing one might think; but then my father already suffered from dementia. What could be worse than that?

"Sheila's mother has cancer," he said.

"Oh, I'm sorry."

My brother then began a lengthy explanation of Sheila's mother's prognosis. A good sister might have left her reverie and followed his thoughts. Instead, I found myself back seven years ago when I was still married to Ray and standing on the ridge with my parents at the cemetery.

"Did you notice that the plot is three caskets wide?" Mama had asked. "I'm here." She pointed to the left, then right. "And your father's there."

The light slowly dawned. Mama thought I would have been more grateful than I was that she and Papa had bought an extra plot just for me. Nevertheless, I was, indeed, ungrateful. After I'd spent thirteen years building a life for myself out west, why on earth would I want to be buried in between them? Was I expected to referee their fights after we were all dead?

"What made you think this was a good idea?" I asked.

My father didn't say much; he just extended his arm to indicate the general view from the palisades over the river. My mother had to explain this logical decision to her idiot child.

"Well now, honey, your brothers are married and have moved away. They have wives and families." She patted my cheek. "Well, we just don't know about you."

I thought I knew about me. I was married. Ray and I lived in Colorado. We had Helene, and though it wasn't much, we had a little trailer that we'd bought after a night of drinking tequila at Eddie's Mexican Café. I remember Ray talking back to the late-night TV hucksters. 'Still sleeping in doorways? Brother, that's no way to build equity!'

As it had turned out when I left Colorado, Ray got the "real estate." Now, my only equity was ownership of a rectangular piece of sod six feet long and four feet wide.

On the other end of the telephone, I could hear my brother breathing and I wondered how long I'd been sitting there, phone in one hand and red ink pen in the other, not saying anything. Mentally, I clamored my way back into the reality of my cold, drafty apartment — the present hole I'd dug for myself, rather than the hole Mama and Papa were waiting to dig for me.

"Sorry," I muttered. "Lost in karmic memory."

My brother sighed, and I could sense that whatever he'd just gotten off his chest had allowed him to wind down a little bit. "If she'd just stop springing things on us, it would be a lot easier," he said.

On Thursday both brothers and their wives drove a combined eight hours to our parents' house, but it didn't really seem like Thanksgiving. There was no brown aroma of roasted turkey wafting through the house. No one wanted the gathering to be a burden to Mama. An average day with Papa was challenge enough.

Rather than cooking and carrying the turkey all the way from Missouri, Alan and Jessie brought a spiral sliced ham. Sheila brought a congealed cranberry nut salad that she usually made every Thanksgiving at their house in Maysville. Danny brought a relish tray and caffeine-free Cokes. I'd baked a sugar-free pumpkin pie because I was on a diet again. Mama went ahead and baked a cherry pie because Alan was coming, and that was his favorite, and because he didn't come home often.

"No one else wants to eat sugar free pie," Mama said. That made sense, but still I felt slighted. Even when I did live in the same town as Mama, she never baked me my favorite pie. It happens to be pumpkin.

That morning I'd hustled all our dishes into the car and drove out to the house. When our dinner was ready, however, no one was hungry, so the food sat in the refrigerator while the family sat in the living room — Papa in his spot on the sofa, Alan on the other end, and me wedged between them. A warm breeze stirred the curtains though the opened window and rattled the leathery hanging pin oak leaves in the front yard. Papa pulled his green sweater close to his chest. Mama fanned herself with a newspaper, in a way that combined both waiting and demanding attention at the same time.

My brothers and I eyed each other. Each of us had arranged our schedules so that we could gather. We all knew that we had to "talk about 'things,'" as Mama called them. Things were getting bad. Things had to be decided. Things that had been going on needed to be made known. Things needed to be said.

I scanned the seating arrangement in the room, observing Mama in her chair with her feet on the ottoman, waiting for everyone to be quiet so that she could begin talking about things. She had turned the television down so that we didn't have to talk over top of it, although the rapidity of its flickering rainbow-colored dance kept pulling my eyes toward it despite my attempt to look away.

Mama puffed her cigarette with loud exhales. Danny and Sheila, tight-lipped, sat side by side on the love seat across from her, each gripping their own cushion seat. I couldn't tell if they were mad at Mama for smoking, or for taking up their weekend with 'things,' or if they were mad at each other for allowing it. The silence that ensued was discomforting. Mama kept pursing her lips but never said a word. She seemed uncertain about how to begin to say anything. Helene stretched out on the floor like a puppy that was trying to get someone to rub her belly. Jessie discovered (wisely) that she needed a nap and went back to the bedroom.

"Are we having fun?" Alan shouted at me, as if I were deaf. I rolled my eyes, so he said it again. "Are we having fun?" I'd made the mistake of sitting too close to him on the sofa. He frogged me on the arm the way he used to do when we were kids.

"Whadda you say about a little game of Monopoly?"

I sat on the sofa a little stunned at our awkward reunion and wondering if bruises would come up on my arm. He rubbed my noggin with his knuckles. "Whadda you say, Helene?" he asked my daughter. "You ever played Moh-nop-o-lee?" He made the game sound extra special with this emphasis.

"I don't know," she said.

"Want to play? Come on, y'all. Let's play."

Danny sat where he sat, silent. Mama frowned at this unexpected outcome and kept smoking.

"Come on, Sluggo," Alan said, reaching across me and tapping Papa's knee. "You up for a little Moh-nop-o-lee?"

Papa blinked and nodded, as though he wasn't sure what he had agreed to do. Alan jumped up and held out his hand. Papa shook it, still not sure what he was agreeing to do.

I went into the dining room to clear the silk flower centerpiece from the table and set up the game Alan had found in the basement cabinets an hour before. As children we had spent hours playing Monopoly on a neighbor's front porch, learning the fine art of negotiation through the hours spent arguing, smacking each other's legs, frogging arms, and throwing game pieces at each other's heads until the pieces landed in the bushes or irretrievably in the fissures between the cement porch and the house. Alan always wanted to play again. The idea of owning four railroads, Park Avenue, and all the green and blue properties in a row had fueled his early desire to drive bulldozers, create new housing developments, and become a millionaire with a race horse farm. When I thought back on it, he was a hell of a lot closer to having money than I'd ever come. He was a CPA with a construction firm; I was the butt of his favorite redneck joke. (No difference between a tornado and a redneck divorce; either way you lose your trailer.)

"I'll be the hat," I said.

"Let Daddy be the hat," Alan said and winked. "I'll be the race car."

"I'm the shoe," Helene said.

"I don't want the iron. I don't care if I go last," I protested. "Just don't give me the iron. I gave up ironing when I was in college." Alan put a thimble on the board. I equally despised thimbles, but I'd run out of options.

Alan waved his hands toward Danny, shouting, "Come on over here;" but Danny seemed to shove his fists further into the cushion, staying rooted in his spot. As Alan counted out the money, he told Helene that she could be the banker. She didn't want to be the banker; Alan insisted. "It's an honor to be a banker. It's a position of great responsibility." He said it real fast, as if even he didn't believe it, then he explained the rules to Helene and Papa. Both of them just nodded because neither had ever played the game before. There were too many rules to remember.

Before the second turn on the game board, Alan and I started to argue over whether the money collected from landing in Jail or Luxury Tax went back to the bank or into a pile in the middle of the board. Did Free Parking mean one collected the pile of money tossed into the center of the board, or was it simply a rest without penalty or profit? We asked for a vote. Because Helene was the banker, she thought it should go to the bank.

Papa thought a moment and said "Free the money."

Alan leaned over to Helene and said, "This game teaches you fiscal responsibility. That's fiscal. F-I-S-C-A-L."

"You're such a Republican," I goaded him.

He turned to Helene. "This game prepares you for the game of life."

"Actually," I said. "Life is a different game."

Alan ignored me, focusing his attention completely on Helene. "This particular game is very important. It teaches you how to negotiate for more money," He shook his fistful of brightly colored Monopoly bills. "That's M-O-N-E-Y, and it's something you will need to know about."

"I want some money," Helene exclaimed. "I want all the M-O-N-E-Y." The various piles of white ones, green twenties, and blue fifties had gotten her wound up.

While we rolled dice in turn around the Monopoly board, Mama got up from her chair, rummaged through the closet in the back room where Jessie was sleeping. Finally, she came back into the living room with a new vacuum cleaner.

"It's mod," she said smugly.

The vacuum cleaner bag was bright purple with yellow circles in a daisy pattern. She showed it to Danny and Sheila, taking it apart, opening the zippered bag, showing off the different nozzles, and the tilt of the vacuum head on the carpet. I wondered what she was really selling. Sheila watched Mama in disbelief. Danny's face turned as red as my no-account deed to Indiana Avenue.

"Is this vacuum one of the 'things' you wanted us to discuss?" he asked her.

"I bought it for our new apartment. See how lightweight it is?"

The creeping red in Danny's face turned crimson while the knuckles gripping his sofa cushion blanched white. "And when were you going to tell us about this new apartment?" he asked.

Mama jerked her thumb in the direction of the dining room where Papa, Alan, Helene and I sat around the dining room table. That table had been the centerpiece of my parents' home ever since Mama bought it and the cherry rung chairs that went with it at her brother's going-out-of-business furniture sale back in 1960. Each spring I cleaned and shined every rung of those chairs with lemon juice and olive oil. Tiresome work, but I hoped the effort would one day make those chairs mine.

At the moment Helene was buying up property on Marvin Gardens and Atlantic. She had another green property — Pennsylvania. Alan had a green and yellow property, too. I could see him biting his lip and eyeing her new purchase. I had the deeds in a stack next to me and doled them out as each player made his or her trip around the board. I kept landing on things like

Community Chest or Jail, and I couldn't seem to acquire any property at all.

This game, which I had never won — not even once as a kid — seemed to resemble my life. I had moved into a trailer park, lost the trailer, and then moved into my parents' basement. Now I was going from one low-rent apartment to another with my daughter in tow, paying rent on what seemed the equivalent of Baltic Avenue while the landlord lived on Park Avenue. I never seemed to have enough money to buy into the game. Meanwhile, my brothers and their wives gathered at family holidays to discuss their houses, their gardens, their renovation projects, their jobs, and the beaches on which they vacationed in their condos.

Mama jerked her thumb in the general direction of the dining room table again, indicating that the behavior of one or all four of us sitting there was something she needed to talk about. Her voice jumped quickly from seductive to ballistic. "I can't even get you kids together in one room so we can talk."

"I think we better quit," I whispered to Alan. He had been sitting with his back toward Mama and couldn't see her pinched face.

"No!" he shouted. "We're just getting started. Come in here and talk to us, Mama... Danny... Sheila... We can do two things at once."

He lowered his voice, tapping Papa on the arm. "You're up, Sluggo."

Looking embarrassed, Papa removed his elbows from the table.

"I meant roll the dice," Alan said. Papa lifted one cube and set it back down. He moved the race car four spaces, and then blinked at Alan to see if he'd done that right.

"You're the hat," he said. "I'm the car."

Of course, but after he'd moved the car four spaces, Papa landed on one of Alan's properties with a green house on it, so Alan left the game piece there and charged Papa rent.

"You owe me one hundred and for-tee dollars," he said.

Papa gave him four white one-dollar markers.

"That's a big yellow hundred and two green twenties, which makes one-*for-tee* dollars."

Papa spread his money into a colored fan for Alan to choose whatever he wanted. I felt sorry for Papa. Mama stood in the living room with her two fists dramatically filled with her own hair. This whole game, it seemed to me, was turning into a lot of trouble.

"You're cheating, Uncle Alan," Helene said. "He's the hat and he's landed on the electric company, so he doesn't owe you any thing. He owes me fourteen dollars. That's F-O-R-T-E-E-N dollars."

"There's a "U" in fourteen," I corrected her. I don't know why I corrected her. I guess it's because I'm a mother. Mothers have a way of insisting on having things their way.

"It's my fourteen dollars," Helene insisted, jabbing her finger at Alan and then at me. "Not YOU!"

While they argued over top of him, Papa's eyes drooped, but he held tight to his fistful of money. He made sleepy snockering sounds through his nose. Alan pulled a single one hundred and two twenties from Papa's nosegay of money.

Mama carried the vacuum cleaner into the dining room where we sat. She stood next to me to demonstrate the vacuum's features, lifting it up and down like a barbell. "See how light it is! I'll sell you my other vacuum cleaner," she said. "It's too heavy for me, and it doesn't get down under things, but it'll do a good job."

I must have looked like I was in a buying mood, since I was playing Monopoly.

"I don't need a vacuum cleaner, Mama."

"You need a vacuum," Mama insisted. "The last time I was at your house it looked like it could use a really good vacuum cleaner."

"I have a vacuum, Mama," I said. "I guess I just don't use it as often as you'd like."

Alan rolled the dice; he got a number he refused and rolled again until he got to land on one of his own properties, skipping Helene's property and its hotel rent.

"Mama, Uncle Alan's cheating."

He rolled again and moved the hat for Papa, but it just seemed wrong to keep moving Papa's game piece around the board while he slept. The whole thing seemed wrong to me, taking up the table so that there was no place to eat, having to explain the rules again to Papa when he woke up, or else rolling his dice, moving his game piece around, and counting out his money as if he weren't there. As a joke, whenever Alan landed on Helene's rental properties, he'd take the money he owed her out of Papa's sleeping fist, laughing and wagging his tongue conspiratorially as if he and Helene were in on it together.

Before I knew it, Alan was trying to talk Helene out of charging him the property's rent. Instead he was paying her "lease options," giving her a little money each time he landed on the property, so that he could eventually buy it away from her.

"No!" Helene insisted, starting to cry. "It's a game. It's not real...."

"It is real," Alan said back. "It's *real* estate."

I got up, walked into the living room and stretched out on the sofa. Mama followed and sat beside me. Danny, stoic beside his wife on the love seat all this time, drew his lips down, then puffed out an explosive sentence in Mama's direction. "You called this meeting. So why are we here?"

Perhaps thinking of her wasted congealed salad in the refrigerator, Sheila piped in, "We're obviously not here to eat."

Inspired perhaps by the Monopoly game she'd seen, Mama said, "I know what let's do. Let's all go over to see this cute little duplex I saw in Silver Creeks."

Silver Creeks was the new subdivision across the highway that a local entrepreneur had created from one of those unsightly farms with a collapsing tobacco barn. He'd finally bulldozed that piece of property into submission and turned it into something useful by putting up one-level houses in a ring around the lip of a pond. The contractor set a fountain in the middle of the pond and built cottages covered in vinyl siding. Each cottage had a wooden deck jutting out into the water, as if one could sit there in a lawn chair in the full sun and fish for the rest of one's life.

Hearing the news of new construction nearby, Alan leapt up from the Monopoly table. Ever since he was in diapers, whenever he heard the rumble of a bulldozer or the thud of a backhoe, he jumped up to see what the excitement was about. Wherever there were maples falling over and massive holes being scooped into the earth, there would be Alan.

"What's this now?" he asked suddenly curious.

"It's a retirement community," Mama said. The way she lingered over the vowels, I could tell she liked that word 'community.'

Mama pulled out the real estate pamphlet and began reading the amenities to us — everything from the square footage and size of each room to the optional compacting disposal. "There's a lawn, but you don't have to mow it," she said. "And you can take a little sack of garbage to the dumpster everyday. Let's see ... the dumpster is located behind the activities building. That's where the community can have its parties and reunions. And that's where the laundry facilities are. Your cottage is only one floor, so there are no steps. There's a kitchen, living room, bedroom, patio-slash-sunroom, and a deck…"

On the coffee table in front of Alan, Mama had spread out the pamphlet with architect's renderings, complete with the imaginary geraniums and Adirondack chair that prospective buyers might put on their front porch slabs.

"I thought we were going to talk about Papa," Danny said. "I thought that was why we were here. Why are we talking about real estate?"

"We are talking about your father. He needs help. I just can't do it all any more."

"So, this place is assisted living?" Sheila asked.

"Who does the assisting?" I wanted to know.

"What do you mean?" she asked.

"I mean, is someone going to live with you? It sounds to me like you will have a one bedroom apartment. Do you have a nurse who lives nearby?"

"No, it's not that kind of assisting," Mama said. "It's more like you can stand, or sit on a little built-in seat to take a shower, so you don't have to step over the edge of a bathtub. And there are hand rails in the bathroom. And call buttons..."

"But you'd still be taking care of Papa every day, right?" Danny asked.

It didn't seem clear to me what was going to be all that different from where she lived now — a house she'd already paid off, with a washer and dryer that sat on one floor inside Papa's walk-in closet. She also had an office and two bedrooms.

"You'd just have to see it," she said, then turned to me. "It's cute; you'd love it."

I thought to myself, *If it's cute, I'll probably hate it.*

"C'mon, let's get in the car," Mama said. "Want to drive over and I'll show it to you?"

Alan jumped to his feet, practically dancing. "Let's go see it. C'mon, Mama. C'mon, you guys."

He tried to lift me up by pulling on my arm. I stayed stubbornly glued to the sofa. In the dining room Papa was slumped over in the captain's chair asleep in front of the abandoned board game. "I think I should stay with Papa," I said. "Besides we can't all go."

"C'mon," Mama urged. "I have the key." She jangled the numbered silver key on its key ring in front of Alan's face. "There's a car pad where I can park my car next to the door, and it backs up next to the lake."

"I'm not going," Danny said.

"Okay, Mama. You and I will go," Alan said cheerily. "I'll drive you over." I thought to myself, *So that's why she bakes him a cherry pie.*

While they were gone, I cleared the dining room table. Sheila helped me set it, heat the vegetables and warm the pies. Danny cut the spiral ham. Practically starving, we nibbled on ham sandwiches while Mama and Alan were gone. Helene sat in the living room with the jumble of money, deeds, little green houses and red hotels that I'd scooped into the cardboard box. She began sorting the deeds by colors, the money by number, and making little tract home communities with the plastic houses. She took the race car and drove it across Mama's carpet through imaginary streets.

Danny continued to fume. He'd rearranged his schedule to accommodate a meeting to talk about things, and things weren't going well. "She says 'jump,' and she just expects us all to jump." He and I agreed that the time had come to talk about optional living arrangements, but we didn't think it wise to jump out of the frying pan into the fire. "It's crazy half the stuff she'll do. She's making a big mistake."

The real discussion was about options, and what each option might mean for Papa, for her and for the rest of us. That discussion which we needed to get out on the table never materialized. With the key in her hand, it appeared to us that Mama had already made up her mind.

In twenty minutes she and Alan returned. "Well, you missed it," Alan said, blowing through the front door. "You should have seen the house Mama bought."

"I knew it," I blurted.

Danny sat down again on the sofa next to Sheila. Each hung onto their seat cushion with both fists. His face was flushed with anger as he said, "If you don't wake up, look at the situation, and make some real decisions, I'll decide it for you."

I thought that sounded a little dramatic, but I was willing to stand behind the rest of his argument. Alan sat in the rocking chair, leaning forward, his forearms resting on his knees, as if he was getting ready for a good game of football on the television.

Danny tried to say that he thought moving without thinking through the options would be a disaster. Mama complained that the leaves and branches on her current lawn were driving her crazy. Sheila suggested that she hire someone to cut the grass and mulch the leaves. Mama said the basement was a wreck with all of Papa's things strewn everywhere; it was driving her up the wall. I said, "Close the door. Hell, hammer it shut; there's no reason to go down there." She said the squirrels dropped acorns from the pin oak trees on her sidewalk; she was afraid she'd fall down and break something.

"It's crazy here," Mama said. "Anything could happen."

"Yeah," I muttered. "The natural world is invading…"

The cottage was no safer, Danny insisted. Why drag a man in Papa's condition into a house next to a lake that he could fall into and drown? She was trading one problem for another. Why move into a house with less room, especially only one bedroom, when the clutter in the house where she lived was driving her crazy? I thought Mama unconsciously saw Papa as part of the clutter. When I told her so, she raised her voice. "You never listen to me."

"We're listening," I answered. "We're just not agreeing your decision. Consider the options. You have to think through the consequences of your actions."

Helene stopped walking the tin dog through her imaginary neighborhood to eye me nervously. I was using sentences on Mama I usually reserved for her. Mama put her fingers in her ears, started shaking her head, and humming "Poor Wayfaring

Stranger" to herself. I felt like jerking those fingers right out of her ears.

"And how old are you today?" Danny asked her sarcastically.

Mama squeezed her eyes shut and shook her head furiously. "Shut up. Just shut up. I can't think."

Helene kept looking at Mama then at me, uncertain about how to interpret the scenario. At a loss, Alan began leaning toward the flickering images on the television screen. Patting Helene on the top of her head, he said, "Baby girl, turn that up. You're closest."

Helene jammed her fingers into her ears in imitation. "Shut up! It's too loud in here. I've got to count my money." Now, she scooped up the bills and crying began to put them into little piles.

Sheila sighed and said to Danny, "Ready to go now?"

Danny glowered at Mama while Mama stared back. I got up to check out the sliced spiral ham and Papa in the dining room. The spiral ham was still sitting there but Papa was gone. "Shit," I muttered and went down the hall to see if he'd gone to the bathroom — nope — to his bedroom — nope — downstairs; I called, "Papa?" — nope. Then I remembered how when we were kids sometimes Mrs. Winfrey would come out of her house with a sack of coins and give each one of us a quarter to go through the neighborhood to find Mr. Winfrey and bring him home. Both Mr. and Mrs. Winfrey were long dead.

Outside I began to walk up and down the street, looking for Papa. It felt odd to be walking in front of the houses in the neighborhood, standing and staring into their back and side yards. Once upon a time I had known every tree, storm sewer, or garden in Indian Hills to hide. My brother Alan took it a step farther; he used to sneak into people's houses and sleep inside their closets. I'd asked him about it one time, and he'd simply shrugged, saying, "I guess I wanted to see what it was like to live somebody else's life."

I hardly recognized the neighborhood anymore — willows chopped down, fences erected between each neighbor, open lots built with small vinyl-sided houses amid the brick homes. I couldn't think of a single person who had lived in this neighborhood thirty-five years ago, except for my mother and father. But when I closed my eyes, I could still feel the heat from the asphalt, the way it was when we children played kick ball all summer long. I could feel the cool rising up from the cement porches where we rested to play Monopoly or Clue in the shade. It was as if any moment I could open my eyes and see Terry Ann lobbing a kickball straight at my head, or Ticker's dog Thunder chasing the bicycles we all rode crazily, screaming and zig-zagging through the streets.

But after walking two streets over front and back, I still could not find my father. I came home to get my car keys so that I could start looking for Papa, driving up and down the further streets. As I walked into the living room, I saw most of my family sitting there watching football on the television. Helene was still on the floor counting her money, Jessie had awakened now, and Mama was sitting in the corner of the room with her feet on the ottoman, smoking furiously.

When I went into the kitchen to find my purse, I discovered the basement door open. (I thought I had closed it.) I scooted down the stairs into its cool, mustiness. Tiptoeing around again, I called, "Papa?"

In the very back room I heard a metal filing drawer creak shut. He was there, sitting in the old storm shelter in a fraying striped lawn chair with collapsed file folders all around him. Newspaper clippings had slipped out from their folders; the papers scattered across the linoleum floor. Otherwise, everything was as my father had organized and left it many years ago — his art and history books stacked neatly on the bookshelves, shoeboxes filled with cassette tapes of staff meetings labeled by date, art prints and canvases stacked in the far corner, and on the top shelf, color slides of the various trips around the world that the Bates family had once taken. (He'd bought them at their estate sale.)

I stooped to help my father gather the loose papers all around his feet. "What are you doing?" I asked.

"Sorting out things," he said.

This was what he used to do when I was a kid. Whenever he was upset about work or family issues, Papa went into the basement to organize things, building shelves, or sorting papers. Usually this sorting out also involved a chilled tumbler filled with vodka. Since his third stroke all the decanters in the house now stayed empty.

"What things are you sorting?" I asked. "Maybe I could help."

He looked at me with a sad, tired confusion about him. Before he said anything I could see in his eyes the distance he had already moved away from me. "I'm just sorting things — for my children."

"Which children?" I pried.

He closed his eyes and looked at the back of his eyelids, trying to think, as if he could find their names written on a blackboard there. "There's four of them. Two boys, my daughter, and the little girl."

I rubbed my eyes with the palms of my hands. "Well, maybe I can help you," I said finally, picking up a yellowed newspaper scrap that announced my brother Danny and Sheila's wedding. I showed it to my father. "Do you know these people?"

He shook his head. "I can't read this," he answered. "It's all fading."

"Okay," I said. "I can sort these for you later. Are you hungry?"

Papa nodded. "I thought those people had forgotten to eat anything. And here it is Thanksgiving."

"Let's go eat," I said. "There's some ham sandwiches in the kitchen. Sheila brought cranberry salad and I have pumpkin pie."

"Oh good," he said. "I love pumpkin pie."

Upstairs the rest of the family was already seated at the dining room table eating. "Well, where the hell did you two go?" Mama asked. Apparently, she hadn't noticed or wasn't worried that Papa had sneaked off.

"We were downstairs," I said, fixing Papa a sandwich with a slice of pie.

"I can't keep track of either of you."

Mama's place at the table was decorated with red hotels and green houses lined up around the placemat. "What's that?" I pointed to the stack of funny money peeking out from under her napkin on the table.

"That's her mortgage," Helene answered. "She's bought all the houses in the neighborhood. I'm the banker, so I gave her the money."

"Well, I'm glad to see that worked out," I said.

And it had worked out. Somehow while I was looking for Papa, Alan and Danny had agreed to take it on themselves to fix Mama's real estate problem. Alan had talked Mama down from her buyer's high, confirming her ability to find a really nice piece of property at a great deal, while acknowledging how much family meant to her that she would try not to be a burden on anyone. Then he had thanked her for letting us in on the decision process. Somehow he made it okay for us to accept her right to make a decision and to disagree with her decision at the same time. My baby brother has a way of talking to Mama that neither Danny nor I can manage. Besides that, he belonged to Toastmasters and had taken the Dale Carnegie coursework.

Danny's way to fix things was a lot like Papa's — just do it yourself, get it done, and go on. Danny's part in the plan was to relieve Mama of the burden of having to face the realtor and ask for her deposit back. He planned to spend the night in town and the next day drive over to the Silver Lakes office and cancel Mama's contract, claiming that he had power of attorney. His next plan was to acquire power of attorney. The time had come for Mama and Papa's children to grow older along with them.

My part in the plan was to return to the house as often as possible, since I lived the closest, and begin to sort through the massive amount of things that needed to be sorted, beginning with the basement, and to get rid of what was beyond its use. Soon, Mama would sell the house and Papa would need to live some place where sorting things out only happened inside his head.

It occurred to me that I had the hardest, and the most rewarding, job.

On the drive home, I found myself stopping by the cemetery to visit the gravesite where one day I would be visiting my parents. I stood on the edge of the hill and looked out over the town where I had grown up — the shiny spires of church steeples, the way the sleepy river wound around the city underneath three bridges, the school my daughter had attended, the apartment where we first lived after we'd moved out of my parents' basement. A parking garage sat on the spot that once bore the movie house marquee; but the bakery where Papa had always stopped for cinnamon twists after church, was still in business, celebrating 50 years of inducing diabetic comas.

Helene stood with me, a little impatient and eager to get home. She had the Monopoly board Alan had found tucked under her arm. There were houses to build, properties to buy and sell, free parking to attain, and a plethora of money to count. Besides, the weather had changed, and it was decidedly becoming November again.

"What are we doing here?" she asked.

"Looking over things," I said.

"What things?"

I found myself almost unable to reply. The most that could be said was a wide sweeping gesture of my arm. By it, I meant "all this." I was looking at all of this.

Helene tucked her head and walked back uphill toward the car to get out of the wind. "You know, Mom. It's a cemetery," she muttered under her breath. "Sometimes you just creep me out."

CPSIA information can be obtained at www.ICGtesting.com
Printed in the USA
LVOW101439041211

257720LV00003B/1/P